FUNFETTI FEUD

A SMALL TOWN CUPCAKE COZY MYSTERY

MOLLY MAPLE

MARY E. TWOMEY, LLC

FUNFETTI FEUD

Book Nine in the Sweetwater Falls Series

By

Molly Maple

COPYRIGHT

First Edition: July 2022

For information:
www.MollyMapleMysteries.com

DEDICATION

To Lucy,

Who greets me as if I am one of her favorite celebrities.

ABOUT FUNFETTI FEUD

Not even small towns are safe from sticky fingers.

Charlotte McKay doesn't know what to think when a robbery goes down in Sweetwater Fountains. While the store's owner has always been good to Charlotte, free-spirited Jeanette has remained a creature of mystery from day one. When Charlotte learns that the fountains are worth far more than anyone anticipated, she isn't sure if the small town of Sweetwater Falls is safe, or if the burglar will strike again.

With a business lease on the line and a friend in trouble, Charlotte knows she needs to get to the bottom of who committed the crime...

... Or Jeanette might have to close up shop for good.

"Funfetti Feud" is filled with layered clues and cozy moments, written by Molly Maple, which is a pen name for a USA Today bestselling author.

1

BREAK IN

I keep waiting for the winter weather to break, but April in Sweetwater Falls is still jeans and t-shirt weather, rather than the shorts that are begging me to wear them. I hold my lavender knitted cardigan closed, bracing myself against the rain that hasn't let up for two whole days.

My keys are slippery in my grip, so I make quick work of fitting the correct one into the backdoor of Sweetwater Fountains. The front of the store sells fountains and crystals and things of that nature, while I lease the back of the building so I can make my dreams come true, one cupcake at a time.

Owning a bakery was one of those far-off goals that I never thought would actually come to life. But when Jeanette offered me the kitchen space she wasn't using, I jumped on the chance to open the Bravery Bakery—specializing in the world's best honey cakes.

My smile of gratitude falters when I don't have to turn the key all the way for the door to open.

I frown at the knob, wondering if I accidentally left the bakery unlocked yesterday after I finished baking. "No," I say aloud. "I locked the door."

Marianne's classy sedan rolls into the parking space beside mine. Though the sun isn't awake, we certainly are.

My best friend moseys toward me in full rain gear, the smartie, complete with a purple poncho to cover her chocolate-colored pixie haircut. She grins at me, her big brown eyes greeting me and erasing any amount of grumping I might want to indulge in from getting up so early. "I brought coffee!" she sings, holding two to-go cups in her hands. She comes to a stop a few feet from me when she sees my pinched brows. "I put sugar in it. Enough to give you a cavity on the spot. Not to worry."

"It's not that," I tell her, motioning to the backdoor. "This was unlocked. I know I locked it yesterday."

Marianne's chipper expression falls slightly. "Huh. Maybe Jeanette came in through the back."

I nod toward the parking lot, but I see no sign of the building's owner. Red hair down to her waist, usually clad in flowing dresses from the seventies, Jeanette is hard to miss. "She's not here yet, and besides, she always exits out the front so she can lock it on her way out."

Marianne slowly closes the gap between us, eyeing the

doorknob. "Was it that scratched up yesterday? I never noticed."

I stare at her point of fixation, taking in the gouges to the doorknob with dread. "That doesn't look good. I would have noticed if it looked like that yesterday." I tilt my head to the side. "Though, I didn't notice it just now until you pointed it out, so maybe I'm not as on top of my life as I thought I was."

Marianne takes a step back, her jovial nature falling to disrepair as raindrops streak down her cherub cheeks. "Um, Charlotte, I don't think we should go inside. Call Logan."

I frown at the prospect of calling my boyfriend this early. "He's not awake yet. It's five in the morning."

Marianne nods toward the door. "He'll want to wake up for this. If not your boyfriend, then call his dad. Sheriff Flowers should know things are off. That's his whole job."

I gnaw on my lower lip, worried that I'm making too big a deal out of this, while also being wary that I might not be worked up enough if I'm not already calling it in.

Marianne gages my hesitation and hands me the coffee she brought for me.

Because she's the kind of best friend who not only wakes up before dawn so she can help me in the kitchen when I know I have more orders than I can handle, but she's also thoughtful enough to bring coffee for the both of us.

Marianne digs her phone out of her purse with her

free hand, calling Logan because I'm stuck in the land of indecision.

Except no part of me wants to stand in the rain while whoever or whatever decided my bakery would be an easy mark makes off with my valuables.

"If someone broke in and stole my commercial mixer, I swear..." Even though I should wait for the police, I have to see the damage for myself.

This bakery is my dream, and it's come true before my very eyes with a whole lot of sweat and love baked into every cupcake I sell from my commercial kitchen.

Ignoring Marianne's caution for me to stay put until backup arrives, I move into the bakery that has been my home away from home. I am emboldened by a need to protect this precious dream of mine from shattering.

I don't call out, nor do I turn on the lights.

In the glow of the parking lot's faint illumination, I can see the trappings of my dream job: commercial mixers, huge refrigerator, double stove, and canisters in neat lines along the stainless-steel counters.

Everything is exactly as I left it yesterday when I went home for the evening. I keep my kitchen immaculate because I don't want the universe to think I am ungrateful for this chance to own and operate my very own cupcakery.

I move quietly through the space, glancing around before I throw the lights on, proving to myself that everything, in fact, is just fine.

"Maybe it was a raccoon that messed with the doorknob?" I suggest to Marianne, whose expression looks torn between frustration with me and fear that we are walking to our deaths.

Marianne's whisper is terse as she grips her phone, setting her steaming beverage on the counter beside mine. "A raccoon unlocked the door but didn't come inside and ransack this place? I find that hard to believe."

"There's nothing..." But it's then that my eyes fall on the push-door that leads to the hallway. I point to the muddy spot. "A handprint! I would have noticed that yesterday. Maybe Jeanette came in after working outside on something?"

Every now and then, the free spirit who owns Sweetwater Fountains and so graciously leased the kitchen to me meanders to the parking lot so she can mold a new fountain. She does this if she's using ingredients that might have dangerous fumes.

But she always respects my space and uses the front door, the one that reads "Sweetwater Fountains" in pretty script on the glass.

Marianne's whisper turns shrill as my feet carry me toward the push-door that leads to the hallway. "Wait for the police, Charlotte! Logan is on his way."

But I have to see what might be lurking on the other side of that door. Jeanette's office is back here. The hallway leads to her store, which might have been the burglar's true mission.

I poke my head into Jeanette's office, my eyes widening at the chair that's been tipped over and the safe that's been broken into with some kind of crude tool, I'm guessing. The thing is bent open, with nothing but what looks like old tax documents spilled out.

I move to her desk and open the drawer where I've seen Jeannette stow her laptop. I exhale when that appears to have been left untouched.

"We weren't the mark," I say to Marianne, my voice pinched and squeaky. "Whoever broke in wanted something from Jeanette." I take out my phone and call Jeanette, knowing the ring will wake her hours before she wants to be here.

Only when I make the call, I hear Jeannette's wind-chime ringtone tinkling down the hall. My spine stiffens as I race toward the back entrance of the Sweetwater Fountains storefront. "Jeanette?" I lack the basic elements of grace or caution as I burst in behind the register, throwing on the lights so I get to Jeanette's phone.

Please let her have accidentally left it here.

A scream sounds from behind me, lighting my nerves on fire. Marianne cups her hand over her opened mouth and points to the source of her distress. "Jeanette!"

I rush to the body on the floor of Sweetwater Fountains, noting the disarray of the items. Many desktop fountains have been thrown off the shelves and display tables. A whole rack of necklaces is scattered on the floor.

But the worst sight of all is the body strewn on the floor

of the store. This place was supposed to infuse Sweetwater Falls with serenity, but I'm not sure I will ever feel that again after the sight that fills my vision.

I drop to my knees, horror washing over my rain-soaked face as I grab up the hand of the woman who took a chance on me and made my dreams come true. "Jeanette?" I whisper, horrified that something so terrible could have happened in this small town that I love.

2

SWEETWATER FOUNTAIN FELONY

I hold Jeanette's hand while Marianne calls for an ambulance.

Jeanette's been attacked. My friend has always been good to me. The first time I wandered into her store, she gave me a bracelet to instill me with serenity. She charges me a fair amount to rent the kitchen, and always respects that my space is mine and hers is hers. It's the best leasing arrangement I could possibly have ever wanted.

And it all came to be because of Jeanette's kindness.

I sandwich her cold hand between my palms. Or perhaps I am the one who has gone cold.

Tears fall as I whimper incoherently my wish that this had not happened to someone so fantastic.

Marianne drops to her knees beside me. "Charlotte, she's breathing."

I gasp, unable to parse the details through my shock. "What?"

Jeanette's head has a gash with dried blood crusted around it and caked into her long red hair. The arm I am not holding looks badly broken, bent at an odd angle. But sure enough, Marianne is right. Jeanette's chest is moving. Faintly, but it's there. I try to steady my own racing heart so I can feel for her pulse in her wrist.

A sob cracks out of me as my relief hits the air.

It doesn't take long for the ambulance to arrive, along with Logan and another officer. They gently pry me away from Jeanette.

Questions are asked, but I have precious little information that they cannot discern for themselves by simply looking around at the carnage.

Logan's arms stay around me until Marianne finally coaxes me to stand. I watch the ambulance take Jeanette to the nearest hospital, unable to be the least bit helpful.

Marianne's tears are my kryptonite. The sight of moisture glistening on her cheeks sets my floodgates loose. Logan hands me over to Marianne so he can do his job and get to the bottom of what went down in this trashed storefront.

The store has been ransacked, but a fair amount of valuables are still here. I'm not sure what sort of smash and grab this was, or if that was even the point of the crime. "Was the break-in to steal things, or was it to attack Jeanette?" I wonder aloud, swiping at my slick cheeks.

"Home," Marianne rules. "Let's go to your place and wait for word on Jeanette's status. We're not going to figure anything out today."

"Her eyes didn't open. We both screamed, but Jeanette didn't stir." My lower lip quivers as what looks like the weapon that must have been used to break in comes to light near a puddle of blood. "A crowbar can do a lot of damage."

Marianne nods, her arm around me. "Let's go home. Let the police to their thing."

It's a good plan, but I can't do that. "I want to stay here."

"But Charlotte, we..."

I shake my head. "I'll drive myself crazy if I stay at home. I'm going to work. Might as well be productive if my mind is going to be spinning all day. Until I get word that Jeanette is okay, I'm not going to be able to calm down." I tuck a curl behind my ear. "She's done so much for me. Without Jeanette offering me a deal to rent her kitchen, my business wouldn't be where it is. I wouldn't be as confident as I am. It's all because Jeanette took a chance on me. I... I..." I survey the wreckage with drooped shoulders and despair plain on my face. "Who would do this to someone so kind?"

Marianne gives a few more perfunctory attempts at dissuading me from my mission, but eventually acquiesces to my neuroses. "Okay. Put me to work, then. What can I do?"

We walk together to my bakery, washing our hands

thoroughly because I have traces of Jeanette's blood on my fingers. The memory of what she looked like after the attack doesn't wash away quite so easily, or at all.

I can barely put my thoughts in order, so I'm grateful Marianne straightens me out. She marches to the refrigerator and counts the unfrosted cupcakes, noting how many I made yesterday on a piece of paper before she opens my laptop—another valuable that wasn't stolen or damaged in the break-in.

None of my things were messed with. Not a single cupcake liner is out of place, yet clearly, the intruder entered in through the back entrance, marching straight through my kitchen.

This was a targeted attack—either on Jeanette or her store, I cannot be sure.

Marianne checks my email for the orders, her eyes widening at the numbers that seem to have doubled since last month. "Wow. Loads of birthday parties. You're still doing a free cupcake for birthday orders?"

I nod, but barely process her query.

Marianne makes a list of how many we need of each of the staple flavors I have listed on my website before she realizes she is still wearing her purple rain poncho. She peels it over her head and jots down a number that makes her eyes bug. "You really can't take today off. Not if you want to get the orders out on time. Charlotte, you should have told me it was this many. I could have called in Logan or Carlos to help. They would have come."

I scrunch my eyes shut. "I can't keep relying on you three. I need to build this business, and not on the backs of my friends."

"Actually, I think that's how many businesses start," she counters.

I nod, but then my stubborn streak rears its ugly head. "Sure, but we're past the start-up phase. If this business is going to have legs, I need a better plan for sustainability. I can't keep relying on free labor. That's not a plan."

Marianne doesn't argue with me, though I can tell she wants to. I know she'll say something like, "We really don't mind," or "We love baking cupcakes with you," but I don't want to do things that way forever. I can't grow if I'm constantly scrambling.

My thoughts keep tethering back to the break-in, no matter how much I try to focus on the work at-hand.

We had a break-in. Someone attacked Jeanette, who is the sweetest flower child ever to walk the streets of Sweetwater Falls. Who would do such a thing?

I pull down a metal bowl and set it on the scale so I can measure the dry ingredients more efficiently. My hands move on autopilot, bereft of joy and filled only with empty purpose.

Marianne does her best to draw me into conversation several times, but I can't shake the image of Jeanette's limp form sprawled out in the center of her store.

She's not a person who was born and raised here. Jeanette happened upon this precious small town, as I did, and claimed it as her own. We fully understand that the rest of the world isn't always this precious, this perfect, so we appreciate it this small-town life that much more.

"Does she have family here?" I ask Marianne in response to her query of whether or not there are more cupcake liners in the cupboard overhead.

Marianne's shoulders lower as she takes in my one-track state. "No. Jeanette lives in the RV park mainly for tourists. She has a few plants, but no animals or family in Sweetwater Falls."

"Should we be calling her family? How would I do that?"

Marianne migrates to my side, wrapping her arms around me in a show of solidarity. She scratches my back in a gentle rhythm, as is her way. "I'm not sure. The police are dealing with it all."

I pull out of her hug so I can put my hands to work. I don't like stopping mid-recipe, and I can't shake the image of Jeanette lying on the floor like that.

Marianne works by my side, putting together the fudge frosting because there is always a hefty demand for my double fudge cupcakes.

I'm not sure how long we work in silence, not dancing at all, which is unusual for my kitchen. There's always music playing in the background, hips swaying by the mixing bowls. But not today. We respect the somber mood of the place. My mind spins. I'm missing Jeanette and going over details that don't lead anywhere while I work.

When Logan comes in to say goodbye, I've got one batch in the oven and another tray ready to go in when the timer dings.

Logan is the handsomest man in the entire world, but not even his sandy-blond hair, sea green eyes or his strong form can bring levity to my sluggish steps.

He kisses my forehead. "I'm going to the precinct now, but we'll be in and out throughout the day while we investigate the scene. The bakery can stay operational, but only if you leave the storefront untouched. We want to get to the bottom of what happened as soon as possible."

I nod. "I don't know who could have done this."

Logan swallows hard. "It makes no sense to me, either. Like I said, we've got our work cut out for us."

Marianne hugs Logan and then goes back to her frosting. "I have to open the library soon. Mind checking in on our girl when you get a minute? This break-in is a little too close to home."

By home, she means my blissful cupcakery, and she is not wrong.

Logan's head bobs, taking in my checked-out state with fresh eyes. "Are you alright, Miss Charlotte?"

I mean to answer him, but the only thing that comes out of my mouth are the details I cannot shake from my mind. "I saw a crowbar. The safe in her office is cracked open. There are scratches on the doorknob."

Logan frowns, taking out his notepad so he can jot down anything I splutter that might prove useful. "So, the intruder didn't have a key and broke in through... which door?"

"The backdoor," Marianne informs him while she adds enough butter to stop a horse's heart. "We came in through the backdoor and noticed it wasn't shut all the way, and the knob was scratched up. It wasn't like that yesterday, was it, Charlotte?"

I shake my head, wishing none of this had happened. This is my happiest of happy places. It's a land where only cupcakes, sugar and my sweet goldfish exist. I lock eyes with Buttercream while she swims in her bowl. I wish I knew how to communicate with her for real. She could tell us what went down. If she could speak, she could probably identify the criminal and save us all some time.

"No security system," Logan comments quietly. "Anything else you can think of?"

"Safe in the office," I murmur.

Logan nods. "We saw that. I'm sure you don't know if anything was missing. That's probably a question for Jeanette when she wakes."

Logan tries a few more times to draw me into the conversation, but I'm useless because too many details are missing.

I need to get to the bottom of this.

3

MARIANNE'S BIRTHDAY

When a fourth voice joins us, it's the only sound that can turn my head. "Honey cake, what happened?"

I drop my spatula and beeline to Aunt Winnie. There are few things more comforting than my great-aunt's hugs. She is ninety-one years old but has lost none of her zest for life. Her shoulder-length silver hair frames her rounded face and highlights her sea-green eyes.

Her arms engulf me, holding me tight in all of her five-foot-tall cuteness. "Logan called and I came right over. Oh, honey cake. Just awful."

"I thought Jeanette was dead! Someone broke into our building, Aunt Winnie!"

My great-aunt runs her hand over my back. Even though I am taller with my five-foot-eleven frame, her love makes her seem giant enough to cradle all that is wrong with the world.

Her eyes are moist when she pulls back to surveil the scene. “Marianne, don’t you have to open the library?”

Marianne nods, addressing Aunt Winnie. “I didn’t want to leave her alone, and she won’t go home.” She squeezes my hand. “Charlotte, are you sure you don’t want to take a break?”

I shake my head, returning to the mixing bowl. “No. I’ll be no good to anyone if I’m alone with my thoughts and nothing else in my brain. My hands need to move.”

Aunt Winnie waves her hand toward the exit. “Go on, Marianne. I’ll take it from here.”

I hate that they think I require supervision. It’s Jeanette who’s been through the real tragedy. She’s the one who needs the support, not me.

Logan ducks his head apologetically. “I’ll be in and out, but I have to be out at the moment. I need to check in on Jeanette’s status after going into the precinct to file my report.”

Aunt Winnie pinches his cheek as if he is a little boy. “Go on, sweetheart. I’ll keep an eye on our girl.”

Marianne and Logan exit after promising to call later in the day.

I work without stopping for the next four hours. Aunt Winnie seems to understand that I don’t want to talk about how I found Jeanette, or how violated the whole thing makes me feel, knowing someone broke into our place of work.

Aunt Winnie assigns herself to dirty dish duty, keeping me in clean dishes until she insists we break for lunch.

"I'm not hungry."

"You sound like your mother whenever she was fixated on a project. It doesn't matter if you're hungry. We did what you wanted for the past few hours. Now I get to choose, and I choose lunch. Agnes is bringing over soup from Gus for us." She doesn't hesitate to take control when I'm spinning out. Aunt Winnie is exactly the right amount of pushy, ensuring I don't stay stuck in a rut forever.

I perk up marginally at the mention of the fancy treat. "From the Soup Alleyoop?"

Aunt Winnie produces a small smile. "Absolutely. It's the best soup in town."

I wind down my work, putting out the small problem that I have thirteen dozen orders for the flavor of the month, and I haven't landed on a flavor yet. That's the last time I put "Mystery Flavor of the Month" on the website instead of waiting until I can commit to a flavor.

Something will come to me. It always does.

But it needs to come today since I have several people showing up at my business tomorrow morning at nine o'clock to pick up their orders.

When Agnes knocks on the backdoor, her eyes are wide with worry. "Oh, Charlotte! Marianne and Winnie told me everything. You poor dears!" Agnes' short, white hair is swept back with two pearl clips, permitting a few ringlets to frame the round shape of her pretty face. "Gus sent over enough soup to drown your sorrows in. And I'm under strict instructions that if you happen to need more, to tell him immediately, so he can send over another quart."

My distracted nature settles as the sweetness of Agnes' boyfriend sizzles in my chest. "That's nice of him."

Agnes sets the to-go bag on the counter and pulls out several cups with plastic spoons for us. "Walk me through it. What happened?"

I shake my head. "I don't think I can. I'm too upset. Is it okay if we don't talk about it right now? I'm trying to clear my head, and it's an uphill battle."

Agnes nods quickly. "Of course. The whole thing sounds just awful. Why, Marianne told me Jeanette looked dead when you found her. She..." But Agnes stops short, clamping her hand over her pink-painted lips. "I'm doing the exact thing you just said you didn't want to do. I'm talking about it when you already said you were overwhelmed with it all." She waves her hands in front of her face. "Somebody, change the subject."

I would, but I'm coming up empty as I pop open the top of the cup of Manhattan clam chowder. I'd never tasted that variety of clam chowder before I spent a few weeks helping Gus out at the Soup Alleyoop. I'd thought all forms of clam chowder were disgusting, and usually,

I'm right. However, Gus has a magic about him, a passion for soup that rivals my obsession with cupcakes.

I take my cup in my hands and sink to the floor of my cupcakery, which thankfully, I always keep decently clean. "I can't think up a cupcake flavor of the month."

Aunt Winnie pats the top of my head. "It'll come to you when you're ready for it."

Agnes takes out a few napkins. "I've always been partial to your red velvet cupcake. So delicious."

I nod noncommittally without verbalizing that it needs to be a new flavor on the menu, not one that I've done before. I've got my standard three: vanilla latte with a butterscotch buttercream frosting, a vanilla bean cake with a vanilla bean cardamom glaze that's topped with Italian meringue, and a decadent double fudge cupcake. I leave space on my website for a flavor of the month, which so far has eluded me.

Aunt Winnie clasps her hands together. "I know what we can talk about. Marianne's birthday is next week. I was hoping you two would use the gift certificates we got you a while back."

"Gift certificates?" I inquire, marginally joining the conversation.

Aunt Winnie drums her fingernails atop my head as she stands beside my spot on the floor. "Do you remember the present we got you two for being our junior members of the Live Forever Club? We got the two of you flying lessons."

I blanche, my eyes widening. I think I pushed that out of my mind, but the memory comes forcefully back into my awareness. “Oh, right. Um, I’m not sure Marianne will want to face her own mortality on her birthday.”

Aunt Winnie’s mouth pulls to the side. “Fair enough. If not flying lessons, then I vote for a party in the library. Not just the Live Forever Club, but everyone.”

“Everyone who?”

Aunt Winnie rolls her hand out in a circular motion. “Everyone-everyone. The whole town. We have exactly one favorite librarian. She deserves a party. We all do.”

My mouth falls open. “You want to throw a party and invite everyone in Sweetwater Falls?”

Agnes claps excitedly. “Oh, that’s a great idea! The library can be the setting because there’s plenty of seating and space for everyone. We should do an outdoor event, too. Something for the kids.”

I balk at the plan the two of them come up with on the fly and then roll with as if it’s gospel. “You’re talking about taking over the library on a Sunday and turning it into a massive birthday party?”

“A town party for Marianne.” Agnes gets out her phone and calls Karen—the third member of the Live Forever Club. In a few short sentences, she fills Karen in on the birthday party that now has a date, a location, and a theme.

More details are added to the list to truly make it an event. “Come dressed as your favorite storybook character.

Prizes for the top three, chosen by the birthday girl herself," Karen announces on speaker. "I'll think of something for the outdoor activity. Maybe I'll call Rip to see if he's got any suggestions. Our Town Selectman always has something wacky up his sleeve."

I pinch the bridge of my nose as I stand, migrating to the far counter to the notepad I always keep handy. I set my half-eaten cup of soup on the counter so I can focus. "I need to write these details down." I jot the bullet points that have come together far faster than anything I might be able to plan on my own. "I can handle the desserts." I turn to Agnes. "What's Marianne's favorite cake? I know she loves cheesecakes, but what about her favorite birthday cake?"

Agnes raises her finger in the air because she is confident of the answer. "Funfetti!"

My brows pinch. "Funfetti is Marianne's favorite birthday cake?" I've never met an adult who claimed that as their desired birthday treat. "Are you sure?"

Agnes nods. "Marianne had funfetti every year growing up, packed with so many colorful sprinkles, it had more sprinkles than frosting."

I make a note to buy more sprinkles than necessary, just in case. "Done. How many guests are we thinking?"

The long pause tells me the number is going to be more than I can handle.

Aunt Winnie shrugs. "However many people were at the last town event we can probably count on to show up to this one. We'll have Carlos, Logan, Fisher, and Sheriff Flowers bust out their grills. Hot dogs for all, and I'll start up a chain of people to bring sides and condiments."

A small smile tugs at the corner of my mouth. "A picnic potluck at the library with everyone dressed as their favorite literary character?" I envision the setup and know this is exactly what Marianne would like for her birthday, minus all the attention. "I think it sounds perfect."

Aunt Winnie grins at me. "That's our style."

I marvel at the women I can't believe I ever lived my life without. "Man, you three could rule the world. Feel like solving my conundrum? I can't think of a cupcake flavor of the month."

Agnes taps her temple. "I think we just did. It's the Marianne Special. Funfetti cupcake with too many sprinkles."

I chuckle at the suggestion. "I guess it's decided, then." I don't relish the idea of doing something so simple for the flavor of the month, but I don't have the energy to argue or come up with something more elegant.

Agnes' hands clasp over her heart. "Oh, I just love sprinkles."

The three of them divvy up responsibilities for the party, while I try to wrap my mind around adding cupcakes for the entire town onto my workload.

4

BETTY'S RETIREMENT PLAN

It was three days before the tape came off Jeanette's office door and store, permitting me entry to the rest of the building. I have no real cause to meander into her business, other than sheer curiosity.

Jeanette is in a coma, I've learned, so she cannot identify her attacker, nor can she come to clean up her store.

I don't have much time to spare, given that my cupcake orders are growing every week, but I cannot let Jeanette come back to a mess. No one deserves to see their dreams shattered and broken.

When I would normally finish for the day, instead of heading home in my red sedan, I move to the front of the store, taking in the disaster that once declared unfettered peace to passersby.

Whatever details my mind preserved were dulled to suit my tolerance for anxiety. I recall none of the larger fixtures being toppled over. Whole concrete fountains have been smashed and left in pieces on the floor with water spilled out and poorly cleaned up.

I move to the supply closet in the hallway between my business and hers, taking out a mop and bucket. I keep silent, unsure what steps need to be taken next and in what order. My want to mop is disrupted by the total lack of available floor space, since there is so much debris littering the floor.

Perhaps the garbage bin will be of greater use.

I run my hand over my face. My feet are killing me, and my arms are already about as useful as spaghetti as I meander toward the garbage bin and drag it to the center of the floor.

Bags won't be necessary since every shard and jagged rock would tear right through the plastic.

I lift a chunk of concrete that Jeanette poured and mixed by hand. It used to be a birdbath with jade stones around the well. The pricey fixture sat in the window.

When a knock sounds at the locked front door, I stiffen.

The very clear sign of "Closed" has been displayed in the front window for the past few days, in case word didn't travel fast enough.

I move toward the front window, peering through the glass to a face I sort of recognize. "Betty?"

Rip's wife has been to every town function, but I have

yet to shake her hand and engage in a real conversation with her.

The woman in her late sixties waves at me, motioning for me to open the door.

I point to the sign, not unkindly. "The shop's closed, actually." I cast around to the mess that can be seen through the glass door. "Jeanette's had a bit of an accident, unfortunately."

Betty nods, tapping her fingernail on the glass. "I heard about it. That's why I stopped by."

I can hear her, but only just. Though I don't work here and shouldn't be opening the door to the public, I turn the lock and crack the door just a smidge so I can hear her better.

Betty has a pleasant demeanor, clad in a bright pink jogging suit paired with a sad smile. "I stopped by to see if I could help clean up the place. I heard it was quite the mess in there. I didn't want Jeanette to get back on her feet and return to a disaster."

I purse my lips. "I had the same idea. The police tape came down this morning, so I suppose it would be okay if you came in to help out." I glance around the place, wary of a sweet old woman coming in and possibly getting cut on something. "There's a ton of jagged edges, though, so you might want to come back after I've finished with the big pieces."

I let her in, taking her gasp in stride. I haven't let myself react in any way other than putting myself to use yet, but

Betty's grief over an establishment like Sweetwater Fountains being trashed is a hit that settles in my chest. Her palpable grief reminds me to be sad when all I want to do is brush my feelings under the rug under the guise of hard work.

I lower my chin. "Be careful where you step. Her fountains were smashed, and some of these pieces could go right through a shoe."

Betty covers her mouth with her hand. She blinks at the mess for several seconds before she speaks. "We need work gloves. Work gloves and a second trash bin."

I nod but know I don't have gloves at home.

Betty holds up her finger. "I don't want anyone to see her store like this. I'll be back with work gloves and a second trash bin."

I nod, grateful for the help. "I'm not sure where to start."

Betty chuckles, but there is no joy in the sound. "Let's start with the big pieces that are obviously trash. The gemstones can be reused, so set those aside in a pile." She points to a larger fountain in the back corner of the store. "That is her most valuable piece. Those gems are real. I call that one the fancy fountain. I can't believe the criminal didn't take it."

"Maybe it was too heavy to move."

Betty runs a hand over her face. "I'll be back to help in a jiff."

I nod, thankful for the direction. When she exits, I lift

only the larger chunks of the broken artifacts, setting them in the bin until it is almost too heavy to move. I drag the thing to the dumpster out back in the parking lot and empty it, sweating as I heave the solid chunks over the edge.

I make sure to give the fancy fountain a wide berth. It is as tall as I am, and the lip has large gemstones all the way around inlaid into the sparkly concrete vessel. I've noticed the thing before, but now that I know it is worth every penny of the steep price tag, I treat it with due deference.

I make three more trips to the dumpster before Betty returns, armed with two pairs of work gloves, a spare garbage bin and two paper cups of tea.

I take the cup and sit down at Betty's behest. "Thanks for the tea. That's thoughtful of you."

Betty smiles at me, setting her cup down and picking up where I left off, lifting medium-sized chunks of concrete into her bin. "I'm not sure we've formally met, but I order your cupcakes often, so I feel like I know you."

She doesn't comment on how sweaty I am, that my hair is a frizzy mess of strawberry blonde curls, or that I have a chocolate frosting stain across my shirt sleeve.

"Then I should introduce myself. I'm Charlotte McKay, Winifred's niece."

Betty chortles. "Winifred is a card, that's for sure. She's always up to something fun. I got the invitation to Marianne's surprise party for next week. Sounds like fun."

"Should be. Marianne deserves to be celebrated. I'll be making the cupcakes for the party."

Betty tilts her head to the side, studying my demeanor that has significantly less pep than I usually possess. "You're doing all that *and* your usual cupcake orders? How many employees do you have? That seems like a lot of work."

I run my hand over my face, mopping the sweat from my forehead before I take another sip of the fragrant tea. "I don't have employees, but Logan and Marianne help me when they can."

"That's nice of them. Marianne's going to make her own birthday cupcakes for her surprise party?"

I frown, not having thought that through. "I suppose that wouldn't work. I'll tell her not to come by next week and I'll do the baking myself. It's not a big deal." Though, as I say this, I don't believe myself. "Logan can help me."

She leans down and lifts a larger chunk that belonged to a standing fountain. "Isn't Logan kind of busy with the investigation of who attacked Jeanette? Will he have the time to help you?"

I want to cry, but I know that's not the way to get myself out of this mess. I'll have to bake my way out, which is nothing new. "You're right. I'll do it myself. It'll be okay."

Betty drops the chunk into the bin and then starts putting debris into the second rubbish container. "I've spoken with at least five people who are all hosting out-of-town guests for Easter or Passover in the next week or two.

You're telling me that you can fill all those orders *and* do Marianne's party on your own?"

Pressure builds behind my eyes at her repeated question. "I can get it done."

Betty's fists move to her generous hips. "How many ways do I have to hint that I want to work for you?"

I freeze, certain I heard her wrong. "What?"

Betty leans against the closed front door. "I retired last month. Thirty years working as an accountant, and now all I do is clean my house and listen to everyone else's ambitions because I have none of my own." Her face sours. "That's not me. I always have things to do. But since I retired, life is so..." She tilts her chin up, fishing for the right word. "...so boring!"

I choke out a laugh at the twist I didn't see coming. "You just retired after thirty years as an accountant, and now you want to work in a bakery that was just broken into this week?"

Betty nods firmly, as if I didn't say anything strange at all. "That's right. I've had a month to do nothing, and I'm going crazy! I don't want to be Rip's helper, setting up for town events and not having anything of my own to take up my days."

"Do you..." I don't know how to phrase my question, since she is in her sixties, and I don't want to be disrespectful. "Do you bake? Is this a passion of yours?"

Betty shrugs. "I've got three kids and seven grandkids. I can follow a recipe. I have an excellent work ethic, and I want to do something different. I could find accounting work, but I don't want that. I want to get my hands dirty."

I motion to the store. "You picked the right place." I lean forward, trying to force my brain to do math. "Give me a few minutes to think about what I can afford. I honestly do need an employee. I can't keep leaning on Marianne and Logan forever. It would be part-time. You'd mostly be following recipes that I can walk you through until you're comfortable with them. How many hours a week are you thinking?"

Betty shrugs. "However many you need. Maybe we should start out with two days a week? Get my feet wet before I jump into the frying pan?"

Gotta love a good mixed metaphor.

I massage my temples, thinking of the money currently in my business bank account, and what I can count on to come in regularly. I rattle off an hourly wage that might be insulting to an accountant who's been working for thirty years, but seems fair for an entry-level baking position.

Betty barely processes the offer before she accepts it. "I'll take it. Tonight, I'm going to clean up Jeanette's business. Can I start baking with you tomorrow?"

I nod, marveling at the help that came to me right when I needed it most. This town is always surprising me.

I finish the tea Betty brought and get back to work, hauling out the filled garbage bins so Betty doesn't have to labor with them.

As the hours pass, I find that I don't mind working with

Betty. She hums to herself while she works, chatting pleasantly often enough to form a connection, but not incessant enough to be exhausting. I find that I don't mind her company one bit.

By the time the two of us leave for the night, it is well past dinnertime. The store is far from clean, but the worst of the debris is cleared away.

"See you in the morning, Boss," Betty waves with a smile touching her pretty hazel eyes.

As I dump my body into my red sedan, gratitude rolls through me. Even though Jeanette's store isn't perfectly cleaned, she has help getting on her feet.

And now, thanks to Betty, so do I.

5

BAKING WITH BETTY

I recall Aunt Winnie heating me up a plate of roasted chicken with asparagus and a salad.

I recall showering the dust, chocolate and dirt off me.

I don't recall the steps I took from the shower to the bed, but when my alarm rings what feels like three hours too early, I groan as I roll off the mattress.

I keep my footsteps quiet as I meander through the house before dawn, knowing I have a full day of work ahead of me, and I don't want to wake Winnie prematurely.

One of us should be able to sleep in.

I drive to my store in the dark, unsure how to set about training a woman who has more time clocked in a kitchen than I've been alive.

I can tell I was out of it yesterday since I didn't properly put away the baking soda or the cleaned dishes.

I feed Buttercream, greeting my goldfish with what I hope is a good enough representation of a smile. "Good morning, Buttercream. Did you see the new doorknob Logan put on for me yesterday? Nice, right? So thoughtful. Poor guy's got his hands full with the investigation, but he still makes time to help me out."

Buttercream flicks her tail in response, which I take to mean, "Logan's the greatest."

My goldfish and I always agree on the important things.

I straighten my eight-inch knitted doll of Bill, who is one of my favorite residents of Sweetwater Falls. I wrap his soft, stuffed arms around Buttercream's bowl, pretending that my surly former employer from when I worked at the diner is capable of getting all snuggly for a cute pet.

Bill hates that I have this doll, which is probably one of the many reasons why I love it so much.

I set about my normal tasks after I take inventory of what I've done so far, and what still needs to be completed. Today I need to work on cake pops—a product I only sell to the businesses in Sweetwater Falls. It's going to be a steep learning curve for Betty, since cake pops require a little more finesse than cupcakes, but when my cheery new employee shows up at nine o'clock with two paper cups of tea, I have faith that she can tackle just about anything. She's got that optimistic can-do way about her that makes me want to hug her simply for being born and blessing me with her presence.

"Can I watch you make one batch first? I've never made cake pops before."

"Absolutely. Watch as many times as you need. And mistakes happen here, so don't worry if the first few times the cake droops off the stick. The consistency is more art than science, so it takes a few tries to get the hang of how moist it should be."

Betty is a fantastic student, taking actual notes on a pad of paper she brought with her. She asks questions on occasion, clarifying the steps when I get too in my head and forget to narrate my actions.

When she gathers up the confidence to work beside me on her own batch, I find that I don't mind her company at all. She hums while she mixes her hands in the cake and frosting to crumble it together.

Betty has a lovely voice. It soothes parts of me that have been tightly wound since I found Jeanette on the floor of her own store. Betty hums showtunes quietly, and I find the whole thing pleasant and relaxing.

"Did you always want to be a cupcake baker? You seem to really love it."

My features soften while I get my hands sticky right alongside her. "Always. When I lived in Chicago, I was experimenting with recipes all the time, but it wasn't until I moved in with Aunt Winnie that I gathered up the courage to actually go for it. She's got that way about her that makes you forget why you've been stalling on believing in yourself."

Betty chuckles. "She certainly does. It suits you, this kitchen."

I cast around my happy place, agreeing wholeheartedly. "How about you? Were you all about accounting when you were younger?"

Betty chuckles as she mixes by hand beside me. "I can hardly remember that far back, to be honest. I wanted to be a ballerina for a while, but my parents couldn't afford lessons, so I took to the more cut and dry academics route."

I pause, turning to face her. "You realize you can do that now, right?"

"Do what?"

I motion with my goopy hand. "Take ballet lessons. If that's what you wanted when you were little, but you couldn't make it happen, what's to stop you now?"

Betty chortles. "You sound exactly like your aunt: fearless and optimistic, which is just the sort of thing Sweetwater Falls needs." She shakes her head as she adds a dollop more frosting. "I'm afraid my ballerina days are well behind me. I'm in my sixties, after all."

I don't want to come across as argumentative, but I really can't let this rest. "I'm sorry you didn't get to be a ballerina. I think you would have made a fine one."

Betty bumps her generous hip to mine, giggling at the possibility of her life taking a vastly different turn. "I met Rip when I went to college. I was the first woman in my family to get a degree. No regrets."

My head bobs. “That’s a good credo to live by. No regrets, indeed.”

I take my time showing Betty how to dip the cake pops after they’ve been formed. We start off with the simple emoji designs since they don’t have intricate piping or complicated colors that have to be just so.

While we dip our sticks into melted chocolate, Betty keeps her eyes on her task while she chats. “No word yet on Jeanette waking up?”

“She’s still in her coma,” I report unhappily. “But Logan said there isn’t swelling in her brain, so once she wakes up, she should be… She should still be herself.”

“That’s good to hear. And they still haven’t found the person who did this to her?”

I shake my head. “Not so far. For all the carnage, there weren’t a whole lot of leads. Until Jeanette wakes up, the police are limited in suspects. No one has it out for Jeanette. And the fancy fountain was left untouched, which is the most valuable item in there. I have no idea what happened, or why.”

“Agreed. She’s a gem, and whoever did this is horrible. Jeanette came here when she was around your age and never left. She always has a kind word for anyone she meets, and she gives away more items than she sells some days.”

“That sounds like our girl.” I hold up my wrist to show off the one piece of jewelry I rarely remove. “She gave me this bracelet the first time I met her.”

"That's our girl, indeed."

"My list of suspects is zero, which I hope isn't what the police are working with."

Betty shrugs evasively. "Well, not every foul deed is done out of hatred. Sometimes it's greed or control. Sometimes it's just plain being a horrible person, which means even our Jeanette can be a target."

"If no one hates Jeanette, and no one in Sweetwater Falls is a horrible person, then who might be driven by greed to attack her?"

Betty looks at me as if I am purposefully being naïve.

"What?"

"I love that you have a sweet heart. Gives me hope for the next generation."

"Am I overlooking something?"

Betty motions around us. "This space is prime real estate, Charlotte. I don't know if you're aware, but businesses tend to do well in our town. I don't want to brag out of turn, but Rip is always putting on grand events that draw in plenty of new customers for local businesses. Jeanette isn't one who is likely to sell her business or move her space. If someone wanted to open a storefront and she didn't want to sell, it might have gone south faster than anyone could have predicted."

I stop all movement, giving Betty my full attention. "Do you know something I don't?"

Betty's neck shrinks. "Just gossip." Her eyes dart to the door. "And seeing it with my own two eyes."

Possibilities should be flipping through my head, but no one comes to mind who might fit the description of an angry murderer who wanted to lease the spot where Sweetwater Fountains does business. "You're killing me, Betty. Spill it."

And just like that, our pleasant, sugary tutorial turns into an investigation that takes on a mind of its own.

6

HOT COMMODITY

When Marianne comes in to visit me on her lunch break, I am no closer to digesting Betty's suspicions.

Marianne balks at Betty. "You saw what?"

Betty's neck shrinks. She keeps her voice quiet, as if she is afraid of being overheard. "It might not mean what we think it means. Maybe it was just a frustrating conversation that got out of hand. I didn't witness the whole conversation, just part of it."

Marianne lays out the facts as they have been explained to us. "You saw Lydia, the receptionist at The Snuggle Inn, yelling at Jeanette last week?"

I chime in. "You heard her say that Jeanette was just being stubborn, and she would regret not kicking out the Bravery Bakery so she could rent to Lydia instead. You heard her say that?" I know I heard Betty correctly the first time, but I need confirmation.

Betty nods, looking as if she wished she hadn't said anything to us. I can tell it makes her uncomfortable to be this near a scandal. "I'm sure Lydia didn't attack Jeanette and put her in the hospital, but the whole thing was so surreal. I didn't know Lydia wanted to open a bakery. I didn't even know she baked!" Betty shakes her head at herself. "Just goes to show how little I know about the people in my own town. But now that I'm retired, that's about to change. Can I help hand out the cupcake orders when people come to pick them up, Charlotte? That seems like a good way to get in some face time with the people I haven't spent enough time getting to know." She motions around the bakery. "The point is that this space is a hot commodity."

"Of course you can pass out the cupcake orders for the weekly pick-ups. That's totally fine, and a big help." I take a bite of my sandwich, perching atop the counter so Betty can sit in the spare chair with her lunch. "I don't know Lydia well. She works the front desk at The Snuggle Inn. I know she had a birthday last month, because Fisher ordered cupcakes from me to surprise her. Other than that, I'm out."

Marianne's face sours. "I can't imagine anyone raising their voice to Jeanette. It's like yelling at a sunrise. Jeanette's so sweet."

Betty holds her napkin over her mouth while she talks.

Even in her bright yellow jogging suit, she is the picture of poise and manners. "Jeanette is sweet. She's also not a strictly business type of businesswoman. She tends to go with her gut rather than by the books. She's had offers for years of people wanting to rent out her kitchen, but she never considered any of them until you made her the offer to set up camp here."

I recall the conversation that led to me renting space in the back of Jeanette's shop. The whole thing used to be a hamburger joint before she transformed the dining area into a storefront meant to sell fountains, birdbaths, crystals and the like. "I didn't make her an offer. I didn't even realize that was something I could do—rent just a kitchen instead of a whole restaurant space. Jeanette approached me with the deal."

Betty smiles softly, her hand going over her heart. "That's Jeanette, alright. She doesn't care about the money as much as she cares about the right energy coming into her space. She's got her own way of doing business, and it works just fine for her."

Marianne locks eyes with me. "But I can see how it might not work just fine for any number of other people who might have wanted this space. Watching your dream come true, Charlotte, in the space where they dreamed their own ambitions might come to light has to be a hard hit to swallow."

My sandwich turns bitter in my mouth. I don't like to

think of anyone being cross with Jeanette because she took a chance on me.

I don't know if Lydia was behind putting Jeanette in the hospital, but I do know that as soon as I finish for the day, I am heading straight over to The Snuggle Inn to have a friendly chat with the receptionist.

7

CUPCAKES WITH THE RECEPTIONIST

After a full day of training Betty and a few hours spent cleaning up a little more in Jeanette's storefront, I take a cupcake in a small to-go box and head over to The Snuggle Inn.

The place is cute. There's no other word for it. The shutters are peach and the curtains lace. The whole place looks like a precious little getaway—a place where every big city dweller yearns to escape to something simpler and less harried. The flower boxes are filled with white daisies, making the whole front of the building look like a doll house.

While I usually pay a visit to the chef with whom I have a solid friendship, today I linger by reception, smiling at Lydia while she speaks to a customer on the phone. "Absolutely. I'll send up more towels right away."

She fixes me with a wry smile after she hangs up,

brushing her black bangs away from her forehead. "I guess I'm sending myself, since the housekeeper is on his break."

"Long day?" I ask, hoping to break the ice with this acquaintance.

Lydia sighs dramatically. "All the days are long here. But that's okay." She motions to my form. "Did you want to see Fisher? He's in the kitchen."

"Actually, it's you I came to visit, but I can wait. I see you're busy."

Lydia's dark brows raise in surprise. "Me?" She's got a curvy figure that she fans at the attention, playing it up with a smile aimed my way.

I nod pleasantly. "I tought we could both use a little girl time."

Lydia nods as if she very much agrees that is the perfect reason for a break, and then she holds up her finger. "I'll be right back after I deliver the towels."

I step back from reception, hoping my presence doesn't fluster her.

When she comes back a handful of minutes later, I slide the small pink box across the desk with what I hope is a welcoming smile. "I'm always bringing Fisher cupcakes. I thought you could use a boost today."

Lydia brightens, popping open the lid. "I *could* use a boost today! Thank you. Really? This is for me?"

I nod, glad that she seems pleased at the offering. Then I reach for something underhanded—a boldfaced lie. "Jeanette mentioned that you're a fellow chef, so I thought it might be fun to talk shop with someone other than Fisher." I feather my fingers together. "So, what's your poison? Baking? Cooking? Breakfasts? What do you like to cook?"

Lydia's smile twists as she blanches while trying to maintain her composure. "Jeanette told you that?"

It's my turn to grimace. I'm a terrible liar. I don't know why I thought this should be the route to take with her. "I think she mentioned something to that effect. Did I get it wrong?"

Lydia waves her hands to clear the air. "No, no. I don't bake cupcakes, like you." Her voice lowers. "I actually wanted to open a branch of a burger franchise. Be a business owner." She motions around to the foyer of the inn. "Not that this isn't every little girl's dream job." She rolls her eyes. "But I read up on this food chain—the Burger in a Bag. That's what I was talking to Jeanette about. She must've gotten confused. I don't cook or bake or anything on a professional level. But I do know how to manage a business. I pretty much do Lenny's job when he's not here." She dips her finger into the frosting on the cupcake and sticks the digit in her mouth. "Oh, that's glorious."

"A fast-food chain, eh? That sounds like a brand-new challenge to tackle. Nothing wrong with that." My nose scrunches. "Come to think of it, I'm not sure I've seen any big restaurant chains in Sweetwater Falls. You'd be the first."

Her eyes widen as she holds out her hand to me. "Right? That's the appeal. I wanted to open a fast-food restaurant," she pauses to shoot me a culpable look, "well, in the spot you ended up renting."

"Oh." The awkward silence fills the air when the cards are laid out on the table. "I didn't realize I stepped on your toes when I moved in there. I'm so sorry. I had no idea."

Lydia waves off my concern. "I know you didn't. You're new in town, and I only told Jeanette about my plans. There's no way you could have known. But I had my heart set on that place. It used to be a hamburger joint, you know, before Jeanette turned the dining area into a fountain store with all that hippie stuff. And the branch I would open sells hamburgers. I thought that would be nice, since that was the building's original design."

I nod at her ambition, always ready to support another woman's dreams. "Totally."

"All the franchisee needs is a kitchen. No dining area. I could have a to-go window installed along the back of the building. It wouldn't have bothered Jeanette's business at all since the only parking needed would be for the employees. I still can't believe she didn't go for it." Lydia rolls her eyes. "Said she couldn't 'vibe with that message.' What does that even mean? What message does a burger chain have that is in any way controversial?"

I shrug, unsure why Jeanette passed on the partnership when she was so ready to invite me onboard. "Is Jeanette a vegetarian? That's the only reason I can think that she wouldn't want a burger restaurant in her space."

Lydia grimaces. "Oh, yikes. I think she might be. I

didn't think about that." She scrunches her eyes shut and then bangs her head on the counter over and over in self-flagellation. "Stupid! Stupid! Stupid! That's why she wouldn't rent the space to me! Now I feel bad for getting all mad at her last week."

"Did you two have a fight?" I ask, knowing very well they did.

Lydia scrubs her hands over her face. "Yes. I wanted to know why she wouldn't rent that place to me when it's clear that location has been the golden ticket for your business." She holds up her hands to prove her innocence. "I wish you all the best, obviously, but I'd be lying if I didn't say that I was more than a little jealous when I heard how well your business was doing, knowing that could have been me."

I shove down the bristling I want to do. It's not just the location that lends itself to the success of my business. It's that I have a unique product and the best marketing team ever with the Live Forever Club. I have a support system that lends itself well to taking big risks, and they believe in my ambition.

I was working out of Aunt Winnie's kitchen before Jeanette offered me the space. My business did well without the help of an industrial kitchen. But now that I have the space at an affordable price, the orders are rolling in at top speed.

So much that I needed to hire an employee.

"It's hard to find the right space for a business," I offer, trying to be as kind as possible. "I'm so sorry it didn't work out with you and Jeanette."

Lydia straightens a few papers on the reception desk. "And now she's in the hospital, stuck in a coma because someone broke into her business and attacked her? So awful. Guess I dodged a bullet there. Could have been me."

"You don't think they were after Jeanette specifically?"

Lydia blows a raspberry. "Nah. Who would go after Jeanette? I mean, she and I had words, sure, but no one's going to actually raise a hand to our resident flower child. I'm guessing whoever broke in wanted to steal from the register."

I can't say that Lydia is completely crossed off my list of suspects, but I'm moving away from believing that she would attack Jeanette so cruelly. She readily admitted to verbally sparring with Jeanette.

Sometimes people argue. It doesn't make them killers.

Then again, if Lydia was willing to yell at Jeanette, what else might she be willing to do to secure the location of her dreams?

"This town shuts down pretty much completely at night," I remark. "It stinks that no one saw anything. I have no idea who could have done that to Jeanette." I motion around the foyer. "Did you see anything suspicious that evening? You work here. Anyone out of the ordinary check in?"

Lydia's neck shrinks. "I'm not sure. I was off that night." She leans in. "Can you keep a secret?"

I crane my neck toward her. "Hit me with it."

I brace myself for some damning evidence that places her smack near the scene of the crime. Perhaps she has some weapon soaked in Jeanette's blood at the ready.

But a blush sneaks over Lydia's features. "I took the day off, so I wasn't here. Fisher asked me on a date. Can you believe that? I mean, I didn't know it was him at first. Left me sweet little letters for weeks, and finally asked me out so I could meet my mystery admirer."

I rear back, completely caught by surprise. "Are you serious?" For the moment, all thoughts of getting to the bottom of the attack go to the back of my brain. "That's so exciting! I had no idea!"

Lydia's eyes are wide, her hands going to her cheeks. "I didn't either. I mean, we've worked at the same place for years, and it's always been cordial between us. Nothing more than the occasional friendly chat. Then he does this romantic secret admirer thing. Now all these little signs keep popping up in my memory that I completely missed while they were happening."

My body lifts so I am bobbing on my toes. "Tell me everything!"

Lydia fans her face. "He sent me cupcakes from your shop for my birthday. Looking back, I don't recall him doing that for anyone else who works here. He makes me lunch every day, something off the menu usually. I never thought anything of it. I mean, Fisher's a brilliant chef. But now that I've been thinking about it, I noticed that everyone else on staff gets something on the menu. I'm the only one who gets the special treatment."

I clap my hands excitedly. "That's a sure sign he cares."

A while back, I saved Fisher's life. Since then, he occasionally sends food to my house if I'm sick. If I come into the dining room at the inn, he'll make my favorite drink that's not on the menu. He notices the people who are important to him and shows them his appreciation through food.

I know this because I am the same weird way.

I nod happily, drumming on the reception desk. "All that, plus him asking you on a date? Yes, he's invested. How did the date go?"

Lydia lowers her voice as if gearing up to deliver a national security secret. "Charlotte McKay, you have no idea."

8

LYDIA AND FISHER'S FIRST DATE

I gape at Lydia. "Say that again?"

"Fisher took me to the next state over. It's his favorite dining spot. They make their pasta by hand and grow their own tomatoes in a greenhouse onsite. Apparently, that's where he goes when he needs to refocus or blow off steam. Two-hour drive one way, and we talked the entire time. Like, barely a lull."

"That's amazing! Tell me about the restaurant."

"We went there on Thursday night, which is when they serve their clam fettuccini special. They know Fisher, so they invited us into the kitchen. We got to help shell our own mussels, which isn't a thing I thought I would enjoy, but somehow Fisher made it fun. I got to meet the chef, who speaks only Italian. The whole thing was like stepping into a perfect first date movie."

I clasp my hands under my chin, swooning on her

behalf. "I love it! I'm going to march right back there and tease him about his crush after this."

Lydia chuckles. "I can't believe I didn't put the clues together."

"Thursday night last week?"

Lydia nods. "So, I wasn't at the front desk to see if anyone odd checked in. Though, I'm not sure I would know how to discern something like that."

My first and only suspect has an airtight alibi that places Lydia out of the state with a credible witness.

I guess I'm back to square one, which is hoping that Jeanette wakes up and can tell us who it is that attacked her and trashed her business.

Lydia flips open her appointment book. "No one checked in for just that night, if that helps you."

"It does. Thanks."

Lydia takes a bite of the cupcake, groaning at the flavors. "Any time you feel like stopping by with girl talk and cupcakes, I'm in."

I smirk at her. "Glad to hear it. I'm going to go say hello to your boyfriend before I head out. Have a good one, Lydia."

She waves at me as I move through the dining room and go straight into the kitchen of The Snuggle Inn.

"Charlotte!" Fisher greets me with a harried smile. "How goes it? I've been meaning to stop by to check on you. You must be shaken up after the break-in."

He's stirring a sauce with one hand and plating a

chicken breast with the other. His black curly hair is captured in the hair net, but I can see beads of sweat forming on his forehead.

Instead of standing there while I answer him, I grab up a cutting board and a knife, offering my services without asking permission. "What needs chopping? What can I prep for you?"

Fisher lets loose a grateful exhale. "Thank you! Everyone wants the chicken pot pie today. Can you dice carrots, celery and onions? Two parts onions, one part carrots, one part celery."

"On it." We fall into a graceful rhythm, as we always do whenever he lets me help him. I used to do salad prep when I worked at a restaurant in Chicago. I never got up the courage to push my cupcakes to the owner, so I spent the bulk of my time chopping vegetables.

That is a skill I have carried with me into Sweetwater Falls.

"I'm doing just fine. Jeanette's shop is still a broken mess, but I'm chipping away at it. I'm hoping to make enough of a dent that it's not so depressing when Jeanette comes back to work."

Fisher quirks an eyebrow at me while he bustles about the kitchen. "That's optimistic. Do you really think she'll return to the place where she was attacked?"

The alternative never occurred to me. "I assumed as much. I mean, it's her passion."

Fisher shrugs. "If that happened here, I'm not sure I

would be keen to come back. She mostly works there alone. Even if they catch who did it, what's to stop that from happening again?"

I frown at the carrots while I dice them. "I'm not sure. I hope this doesn't haunt her like that. She needs her store to be filled with serenity. I think we all do."

Fisher bangs the end of his wooden spoon on the pot. "I can't believe Dwight finally cracked and unleashed on her."

My head whips in Fisher's direction. "What makes you think Dwight had anything to do with it?"

Fisher scoffs, his eyes on his work. "Are you kidding? Anything Dwight can do to get a permanent place to rent. He's been talking about it for years—what a waste it is to have a fountain store, and how could such a business possibly make overhead. He approached Jeanette just a couple weeks ago, asking again if he could sell his lawn art in her store, giving her a cut of the sales."

"I'm guessing she didn't go for that idea?"

Fisher chuckles humorlessly. "She told him flat out no. No reason, no negotiation. Just a firm no. He took that about as well as you might imagine. Came in here for lunch one day, complaining up a storm about Jeanette. He said that she must have it in for him to not let him have so much as a table or a shelf on which to sell his lawn art."

I grimace at the new information. "I had no idea. What sort of lawn art was it?"

Fisher shoots me a sidelong glance. "Oh, it's bad. I call

it 'lawn art' because that's what Dwight declares it to be, but it's a mess of welded metal hangers and found objects (also known as garbage). It's all glued together to make windmill-type statues about two feet tall with signs on them that say ridiculous things like 'Don't Fart on My Lawn.'"

I snort at the image that comes to mind. "Are you serious?"

"I wish I wasn't. Every now and then, he tries to sell me one to put on my front lawn. I would buy one just to shut him up. That's what Rip did last year. But then Dwight comes by to check on the sign, wondering why it isn't proudly displayed." Fisher rolls his eyes. "No one around here needs or likes that kind of tacky junk. And the tourists who comes through aren't really looking for bulky two-foot-tall souvenirs."

I've had precious few interactions with Dwight. I've only known him as the guy with all the mascot costumes, but other than that, I'm out.

He dressed up as a giant saltine cracker for the Knock Your Soup-Off event.

He was a lemon for the lemonade competition.

He was candy cane for the Christmas festival.

Adding crazy lawn art to his personality doesn't seem all that strange to me. But placing him in the role of cold-blooded criminal? I'm not sure my mind can make that leap.

I frown at the vegetables while I chop. "You really think it was Dwight who attacked Jeanette?"

"I think that's the only person who might have done something so crazy. I'm telling you. Look at his lawn art sometime. There's no way a balanced person can produce junk like that and call it art." He motions to me with his wooden spoon. "He was talking trash about you a couple weeks ago in my dining room. Said he couldn't believe Jeanette rented the kitchen to you, when it could have made a fine display space for his lawn signs."

I shrink at the unwanted attention. "Yikes. I didn't mean to step on Dwight's toes. I didn't even petition Jeanette for the kitchen. She offered it to me. I'm so grateful. I don't know what I would do without that connection, that space to use. But I didn't know other people wanted it."

Fisher quirks an eyebrow at me. "I can tell you've been talking to Lydia. Did she tell you about the hamburger chain she wanted to open in Sweetwater Falls?"

I bob my head as I move onto the celery. "She sure did. A little birdie also told me that a certain someone asked her out on a date, and it went fabulously."

Fisher whips his head to me. "She told you she had a good time?"

I nod with a giddy grin. "I believe she said she had a *great* time. I even think she was blushing when she told me." I scoop up the dishtowel on the station beside me and whip him with the end of it. "I had no idea you were swooning for Lydia!"

Fisher turns back to his sauce, stirring to avoid eye contact. "I didn't think she would go for someone like me, but I couldn't keep chickening out. I still can't believe she said yes. I thought she would take one look at me when she realized I was the one sending her the secret admirer notes, and head for the hills."

My voice softens. "Why can't you believe she would be thrilled to be on a date with you? You're a fantastic person, Fisher. One of my favorite."

Fisher shoots me a wry look, as if I'm trying to dance around the obvious. "Come on. You know I'm about fifty pounds overweight. I'm nowhere near the good-looking type of guy Lydia probably usually goes for."

I slam the knife onto the cutting board and whirl around, crossing my arms over my chest. "Knock that talk off. She was gushing like a schoolgirl out there, telling me about what a great time the two of you had. Don't let your own doubts about your awesomeness keep you from believing that she said yes to you, and most likely will again the next time you ask her out."

Fisher's neck shrinks. "You think?"

"I think you'd better not pass up the opportunity to date your dream girl. She'll say yes, Fish. She already went out with you once. Ask her again for this weekend."

His voice climbs in pitch. "It took me two years to work up the courage to ask her out for last Thursday!"

"It's all downhill from here." I chuck his shoulder good-naturedly. "You're a catch, Fisher, and now Lydia knows that. Go on out there and ask her on a second date. I've got the kitchen."

Though, truthfully, I don't know what to do with Fisher's sauce or any of the other things that are bubbling around the kitchen, so I hope he makes quick work of securing plans with his dream girl.

I point to the exit. "Now. Right now."

Fisher wipes his hands off on his apron, then mops the sweat from his brow. "She's going to say no. I can feel it."

"The only thing you can feel is the feathers you're sprouting from being a big chicken. Out you go." But I pause him before he turns to march through the dining room. "Hairnet off. That's my only note."

Fisher grimaces, removing his hairnet to give himself a better chance at securing Lydia's affection.

If only he could see how awesome he is; he wouldn't be so nervous.

I get back to chopping, moving onto the onions while my mind drifts back to Dwight and his silly lawn signs.

I wonder if he loves his creations enough to kill for them.

I don't know a whole lot about Dwight, but if I'm going to get to the bottom of who hurt Jeanette, I know I'm going to have to get to know him a whole lot better.

9

BETTY AND JEANETTE

Working with Betty is a dream. I think Marianne and Logan are also grateful that they aren't my only crutches in this business. We have a ton of cupcake orders to fill, but I haven't cried once today because Betty is perfectly competent in the kitchen. After watching me make the double fudge cupcakes while taking notes on the steps, that flavor is officially Betty's to make. When the first batch Betty bakes on her own comes out of the oven, they smell fresh and perfect, dosed with love.

Perhaps the love is a silly non-ingredient that only I can taste, but when I crack into one of the cupcakes Betty made from start to finish without me hovering, I can taste my most cherished ingredient shining through.

"These are perfect," I tell her, admiring her bright orange track suit. She is always dressed like she is ready for a round of speed-walking, complete with bright sneakers and a smile on her face.

"It's your recipe!" she sings in response. "I'm glad you approve. Now I just have to make..." she does the math in her head. "Four hundred more?"

I nod. "You up for the challenge?"

She slaps her hands together as if gearing up for a marathon. "On it, Boss!" She is still getting the hang of the scale, but she handles the industrial equipment just fine, weighing out the flour first.

She hums while she works, which is a feature of Betty that I adore. It makes the whole day that much peppier and filled with camaraderie.

"Betty, can I ask you something?" I say as I start getting out the ingredients for the funfetti cupcakes.

"Anything and everything. To start, no, I'm not single. I married the most amazing man in Sweetwater Falls."

I chuckle at her whimsy. "Glad to hear it. I was actually going to ask why you wanted to work with me, instead of anywhere else in Sweetwater Falls. I wasn't even hiring, but we found each other. I'm really grateful it fell into place the way it did."

Betty keeps her eyes on the flour as she dumps in scoop after scoop. "It's a timing thing, I think. I knew I was unhappy being retired. I'm not one to sit around. I like getting my hands dirty. I like getting up early. I like making people smile. What makes people smile more than a cupcake?" She gets out the baking powder. "I knew I was unhappy being retired, but I didn't put it together that I wanted to bake with you until I came to Sweetwater Fountains to try to clean up Jeanette's shop and found you there. I love Jeanette. To see you sacrificing your free time to clean up her store, all so she doesn't come back to the mess? I knew we would get along just fine."

"I didn't realize you and Jeanette were so close."

Betty motions around the place. "I knew Jeanette when she first opened Sweetwater Fountains. She was new in town but determined that she would put down roots here. I helped her come up with a plan. I even came over a few nights after I got off work and helped her make some of her earlier fountains whenever she needed a second set of hands. Startups give me goosebumps. New businesses make me feel all optimistic about the world. Call me a softy, but I'm a sucker for a good lemonade stand. I love the hustle of a new business. Makes me feel alive." She gives a little jump to display her liveliness.

I smirk at her while we work in tandem. "I can see that. Makes me double grateful you're with me, then. I am definitely in the startup phase of this bakery."

Betty waves off my humility. "Oh, you're soaring. When Jeanette started her business, you have no idea how much she struggled. Now she's doing well because she broadened her inventory to include crystals and birdbaths and whatnot. It used to be only fountains. When she added a few lines to her inventory, her income became steadier." She motions to the stack of cake pop sticks in a bin on the counter. "See, you learned to diversify early on. You have your regular cupcake sales, sure, but you also sell cake pops to businesses. That gives you not only two lines of products, but two entirely different types of customers, so you're not solely catering to people with a sweet tooth, but to other businesses also. It's smart, and it's not putting all your eggs in one basket. When I convinced Jeanette to start talking with business owners outside of Sweetwater Falls, that's when she began to be able to relax." Betty motions to the ovens. "When she leased this space to you, that was the smartest thing she could do for her business. Helps with the rent, plus it brings people in on a regular basis who often stop by her storefront to see what new items she's got."

A smile lights my face. "Really? That makes me so happy. I didn't even think about her revenue climbing because we teamed up. That's great!"

Betty nods. "She's always been a 'go with your gut' kind of girl. She waited until the right person came along to rent the kitchen." She reaches for the salt. "I knew her when her gut was all she had. Such a young woman when she first came here." Her expression twists. "I can't believe someone would hurt that sweet girl!"

Emotion overcomes Betty, but she doesn't break down completely. Her eyes mist over and her voice catches, so I drop what I'm doing and scoop her in a hug. "Oh, Betty!"

"I knew when I saw you cleaning up her place that we were the same kind of woman, you and me. We love

Jeanette. I figured you're the kind of person I want to be around. You could be selling car parts, and I would still want to work with you."

I squeeze Betty tighter. "I'm glad you happen to be able to bake, then. Lucky for us both."

Betty chortles after I release her from the impromptu embrace. "Lucky, indeed. It could have been me who'd caught the business end of that burglar's wrath."

My brows bunch. "What do you mean?"

"I was going to stop in afterhours and take Jeanette out for dessert. Surprise visit. But I ended up going out with Rip instead. Don't think that doesn't haunt me. I could have gotten her away from the mess, so all she would have had to deal with is the broken things and empty register."

I straighten. "Empty register? I didn't realize a burglary went down." My shoulders slump. "Then it could be anyone with the motive of just wanting a few extra bucks in their pocket."

Betty nods. "So sad. I can't imagine anyone in this town would do something so horrible. At least the fancy fountain is still standing. I guess they couldn't tell real gems from the fake ones, which is the only silver lining to speak of."

I tuck that tidbit away, factoring in petty thievery as a potential motive for the scandal at Sweetwater Fountains.

10

DWIGHT'S MYSTERIOUS BOAT

I don't want to connect the dots from money going missing from Jeanette's register to the new boat parked on the street in front of Dwight's home, but I'd be lying if the idea didn't haunt me every few minutes all day long the following day.

I angle my chin over my shoulder so I can bug Karen with my worry. "I still don't understand how Dwight could afford a brand-new boat like that without coming into some serious cash. Seems suspicious, doesn't it?"

Karen Newby chortles at me while I hold the duster aloft in her kitchen. "A grown man owning all those mascot costumes always seems suspicious in my book."

When Karen mentioned she was going to dust on top of her kitchen cupboards this morning at breakfast, I didn't hesitate to volunteer my help. That tiny, wiry woman on a ladder gives me heart palpitations. I followed her home after the Live Forever Club and I ate breakfast at Aunt Winnie's kitchen table. Now I'm on a ladder, moving onto the ceiling fan after vanquishing the dust bunnies atop the cupboards. Might as well do all the things Karen will need a ladder for while I'm here.

"I mean, did he come into a windfall of cash that wasn't the stash that went missing from Jeanette's? What does he do for a living?"

Karen waves her hand dismissively while she watches me work on the two-step ladder. "He's a janitor. Cleans the schools afterhours. Makes a fine enough living to have his own bungalow. But a big boat like that? It's all anyone can talk about today. I saw Delia at the Nosy Newsy, and she was cranking out the gossip on high speed to anyone who would listen. I had to go see for myself, and sure enough, there it was."

"Oh, Delia." The town busybody always has the scoop on the latest and awfulest. "Any idea how he could afford something so lavish?"

Karen shrugs. "Delia thinks he is secretly a millionaire, living incognito in our small town. She's got a whole theory about it. I checked out after she told Frank she's got two notebook pages filled with evidence proving her theory."

I chuckle at Delia's tenacity to go after a story, even when there isn't one to speak of. "Yikes. A secret millionaire dressed as a saltine for the soup festival? That's a stretch."

Karen motions to the lightbulb covers. "Can you get those down for me, Charlotte? Once I get Spring cleaning fever, I take everyone down with me. I can see dust buildup in those covers. If you hand them to me, I can run them through the dishwasher real quick."

Karen turns off the lights so they can cool down before I untwist the covers and carefully hand them down to my friend.

I fish for a change of topic. "Any word on how many we're expecting for Marianne's surprise party?"

"Over a hundred so far, but we're waiting to hear back from a few families still."

My eyes bug. "Will we be able to fit that many in the library?"

Karen waves off my concern. "We don't need to. We're taking over the parking lot. Most people know to either carpool or walk over there. We've got our grillers secured, the cupcakes, of course, and a petting zoo."

I guffaw at her. "A... what?"

Karen takes the first light cover from me without a blink. "A petting zoo. You didn't think we'd have zero entertainment, did you? It's our girl. She deserves a day of fun."

I unscrew the next fixture. "You are amazing, you know that? Marianne is going to freak."

"The whole town will be there."

Though that idea makes me happy, I can't scrub from my mind the very real possibility that we might be inviting a criminal to Marianne's birthday party.

I need to get to the bottom of this before Marianne's special day, or the whole thing could end in disaster.

11

BETTY AND RIP

My time with Logan is limited when there's an open case that demands his attention. While I never complain about his job and he never complains about mine, I'd be lying to myself if I didn't miss him on occasion. Instead of our usual dates, we've resorted to leaving cutesy notes for each other, buried in the flower box of the Nosy Newsy. After a morning of helping Karen clean her house, then an afternoon at the bakery working on Marianne's birthday desserts, followed by an hour of clearing out more debris from Jeanette's shop, I am hoping for a cute little note from Logan, waiting for me in the petals.

My shoulders lower when the note I drop in there sits all by its lonesome.

"Hey, New Girl," Frank greets me. "You coming to the shindig on Sunday?" He stands with his feet more than shoulder-width apart, his black, greasy hair slicked back to reveal his smile with a missing tooth in the front.

"Hey, Frank. Wouldn't miss it. I'm making the birthday cupcakes."

The owner of the Nosy Newsy frowns. "Birthday cupcakes? Nah. You need a birthday cake. Can't go messing with tradition."

My mouth pulls to the side. "You think?"

"I know. Birthday cake for the birthday girl. She gets cupcakes any time she wants, because you're her best friend. Make her a cake this time."

I take Frank's unsolicited advice in stride. "I'll give that some thought. Any idea which literary character you're going to be?"

"Sure do. I'm going to be the clown from Stephen King's 'It'. My sweet Delia is going as Carrie."

I blanch at the gruesome image. "Yikes. I didn't realize people might be going for scary costumes. I'll have to give mine some more thought."

"What's your plan?"

My neck shrinks. "I don't have one yet. Are there any literary characters who wear aprons and haven't brushed their hair in two days? Because I'm thinking I could pull off that costume just fine."

Frank chuckles at me, batting away my worry. "Aw, you'll figure it out. If all else fails, wear your regular clothes and tell them you're the star of some rom-com book."

"Good advice." I fold my arms over my chest. Even though it's nearing sundown, I feel the need to stay out and chat rather than turn in just yet. "Say, Frank? Delia seems to know everything about everyone. Does she know who else wanted to rent the kitchen in the back of Sweetwater Fountains? Apparently, there was quite the line I cut in front of without realizing it."

Frank frowns. "That place? Oh, sure. Dwight wanted it real bad. Then Farmer Ben wanted to rent it a few years ago to turn it into a produce stand. Of course, Jeanette's real particular. Betty and Rip cut her a steal of a deal on that store. She didn't want to bring just anyone in."

I blink at him. "Wait, what? Betty and Rip?"

Frank nods nonchalantly. "Of course. They own that strip. Jeanette's rent checks go straight to Betty and Rip. Betty loves Jeanette. They look after each other, much the same way you and the Live Forever Club are connected at the hip."

My brows bunch. "Why didn't Betty mention that to me? And why is she working for me when she owns the strip?"

Frank shrugs. "Sometimes the work isn't about the money. It's about the company. It's about the fun of it. I love that I make money doing what I do, but I also like that I'm at the center of it all. I get to see everyone and talk to each person who comes by for their morning newspaper. If I owned a block of property and didn't need the money, I'm sure I would still be doing this." Frank straightens a few off-center magazines on his rack. "Betty's good people. If she's working with you at the same place where Jeanette was mugged, I'm guessing she wants the work to keep herself active, sure, but she's also looking out for you. She's making sure the bad guy doesn't strike again and take you out next time. Hoodlums that get away with a crime once are more likely to strike again. Might want to keep an eye on your register, so you don't get robbed, too."

A chill runs through my spine. "You don't really think the person who attacked Jeanette would come back, do you?"

Frank holds up his hands. "Who's to say? Betty might be working for you simply because she loves cupcakes. What do I know? I'm just the guy who knows everything and hears everything about everyone because this is where I work." He motions around his newsstand.

I take in Frank's wisdom, letting it fill my mind with gratitude because, not only do I have my dream job in an apparently coveted location, but I also have an angel in a neon jogging suit looking over my shoulder, watching out for me while we bake together.

Sometimes a girl just gets lucky, I guess.

When I turn to leave Frank to his newsstand, the one face I've been longing to see greets me with an irresistible yet tired smile.

"Well, Miss Charlotte. Fancy meeting you here."

12

LOGAN AND DWIGHT'S FEUD

"Logan!" My arms fly around the shoulders of the one face I was hoping to see.

My boyfriend is without a doubt the sweetest and best-looking man in the world. As evidence, when we break our embrace, he holds up an envelope. "I see we had the same idea. I was going to leave this in the flowers for you." He glances around, noting the absence of Marianne and Aunt Winnie. "Feel like an evening stroll?" He pops his elbow out to me after fishing in the flowers for my note to him.

I loop my arm through his, grateful to feel the warmth of his side pressed to mine. "You've been working long days lately. I'm glad we caught each other."

Logan smirks down at me, his dimpled chin making me blush with how handsome he is. "Look who's talking. You've been sun-up to sundown most days. How's the new hire coming along? Is Betty picking up my slack? I know I'm your Frosting King, but I haven't been able to come by and whip anything up for you lately. This case is…" He shakes his head, letting me know with a labored sigh that he is tired of coming up against dead ends.

I can't say I blame him.

"Betty's wonderful. Did you know she owns that strip? That whole bunch of stores send their rent to her, yet she's frosting cupcakes with me in a windowless kitchen."

"Well, maybe it's your smile that gives out enough sunshine to draw her in." Logan grimaces. "Too cheesy? I meant it, but it sounded silly once it came out of my mouth."

I bump my hip to his while we walk down the lamplit street together. "Just cheesy enough." We walk in-step down the main thoroughfare while the streetlights illuminate our path. "Betty is wonderful. I really lucked out that she wanted to learn to bake cupcakes."

The streetlights have Easter baskets with colorful oversized eggs around the base. There are Easter eggs hanging from the trees that line the streets, and cardboard bunnies poking their heads around the corners of buildings and out from the tops of thick bushes.

Rip really goes all out decorating around here. I love his attention to detail. Anywhere else, the décor might be tacky, but here? It's just plain precious. Practically magical.

"How's the case going?" I ask him. "Betty keeps me

company all day, so I'm talked out. How are you and Wayne holding up?"

Logan's partner is his sounding board when I am swamped with work.

"Honestly, we have no leads. Absolutely none. Everyone loved Jeanette."

My mouth pulls to the side. "I thought it might be Lydia for a minute, because she wanted to rent the kitchen and Jeanette said no. They had a fight about it, actually. But Lydia was out of town at the time of the attack with a witness, so it wasn't her. Now I'm on to Dwight."

Logan's nose crinkles. "Dwight? Wait, you had a suspect, and you didn't tell me? That's the kind of thing I want to know, Miss Charlotte."

I take his mild exasperation in stride. "I only tell you the good suspects. Thought I'd weed out the dead ends first." I chew on my lower lip while we walk. "You don't think the burglar will come back, do you?"

"Who told you it was a burglary?"

"Frank. Maybe Delia told him? I'm not sure."

Logan sighs. "Well, that's one detail out and about. The register was cleaned out. Everything else was trashed, so it looks like it might end up being a standard smash and grab, during which Jeanette happened to be at the wrong place at the wrong time. I don't think it had anything to do with Jeanette specifically; just a plain old robbery."

"I don't need to worry, do I?" I try to keep the insecurity

out of my voice, but I can't help it. Now I'm overthinking it all, thanks to Frank putting that in my head.

Logan tightens his arm, bringing me closer to his side. "I don't think so, but lock the doors for me, will you?"

I bob my head. "I always do." Our arms drop as we turn down the next street, our hands clasping together. "Dwight got a fancy new boat."

Logan chuckles. "I heard. It's all anyone can talk about, which is a relief. It's like Jeanette's attack has been everywhere I turn. Nice to have a change of topic around town."

I try to rephrase my remark to get nearer my suspicion. "I don't know much about boats, but I'm guessing they cost a pretty penny."

"Several," Logan concurs. His steps slow as he raises his eyebrow at me. "Do you think there's a connection between the missing money from the register and Dwight's new boat?"

I shrug. "I'm just looking at anything that someone would need a windfall of cash to purchase. Anything big that came into Sweetwater Falls after Jeanette's robbery. The timing is suspicious."

Logan hangs his head. "Dwight hates me. He's never going to answer me straight if I question him about the boat."

I balk at Logan. "How could anyone hate you? You're wonderful!"

Logan's ears pink. "Thanks. Dwight and I don't see eye to eye about everything. Or anything, come to think of it."

I turn to face Logan, pausing our stroll. "Seriously, why would Dwight not like you?"

"I believe I used the word 'hate'." Logan sighs. "It goes back to grade school. Just petty rivalry stuff. But it lasted longer than it should have. When I applied to the police academy, he did too. He nearly passed, too, but I went on to apply for a job in town, and he wasn't cleared to do the same. We both love this town. I do what I can to protect Sweetwater Falls, and Dwight does what he can to entertain us. But in his heart, he wants the job I have."

"It's not your fault he didn't graduate from the police academy."

Logan shoves his other hand into his pocket while we stroll together down the street. "I'm not sure that matters. I got picked before him when we played baseball. I have a father on the force, to which he attributes me getting a job here."

I grimace at the feud I knew nothing about. "Yikes. I'm sorry. I had no idea you two were at odds."

"If it was up to me, we wouldn't be, but friendships have to go two ways." Our clasped hands swing gently between our bodies while we walk. "And now I have to talk to him about where he got the money for that boat, as if he doesn't have a right to save up his money and buy himself something nice." He angles his chin toward me, a tired look showcased in the moonlight. "Some days I love my job. Other days, not so much."

I bump my hip to his. "Maybe I could talk to Dwight.

Fish around to see where he got the money for that boat. Then you wouldn't have to deal with him."

The corner of Logan's mouth tugs upward. "You care about me." He squeezes my hand to show me he sees me. "But I can't let you do that. Just because something's uncomfortable doesn't mean I'm excused from doing my job."

But my mind is already concocting a reason why I might need to organically seek out Dwight, so I can ask him how he could afford a boat when the only work I've ever seen him do is don a mascot costume for festivals.

13

DWIGHT THE ENTREPRENEUR

Should I have thought through my plan of lightly interrogating Dwight before I stepped onto his property? Probably.

Should I have checked my schedule to see how much work I still need to do before leaving Betty alone in the kitchen for the morning? Definitely.

But as I'm already parking in front of his house, I realize I'm in too deep to back out now. I don a cheery smile and then knock on Dwight's front door. "Good morning," I sing when he opens the door, a surprised look on his face.

Dwight is in a pair of blue flannel pajamas, puzzled at my presence.

As am I.

Why did I think this was a good idea?

Dwight tilts his head at me, his brown hair sticking up on the side. "New Girl? What are you doing here?"

I fix him with a bright smile. "A couple reasons, actually." I hold up one finger. "First is that I was wondering if you were planning on coming to Marianne's birthday party this weekend. There's going to be a live petting zoo."

Dwight runs his hand down his face. "I was planning on it. Did I not RSVP to Winnie? Sorry about that. I'll be there. Me, plus my dad."

"Your dad's in town? Or does he live here, and I just haven't met him yet?"

Dwight shakes his head. He shifts his weight from one slippered foot to the other, his wrinkled flannel pajama pants bunched on the side. "He's coming into town on Friday. He lives in Texas, actually. Comes to visit once or twice a year. We rent a boat, go fishing, see the falls. That kind of thing." He motions to his driveway, his chest barreling. "Only this time, we don't have to rent a boat when we head over to Apple Blossom Bay to go fishing. We can use my new boat. I was thinking of calling it The Ariana."

I nod appreciatively. "Do you know someone named Ariana? Is that your girlfriend?" I know next to nothing about this man.

Dwight's shoulders sink. "No. I thought it would make me sound like I had a girlfriend if I named her something that sounds pretty. Ariana sounds like a girlfriend name, doesn't it?"

I press my lips together, unsure what to say to that. "I don't know the first thing about boats, but perhaps you should wait to name it until you've got a name that makes you feel good, rather than a name that reminds you your girlfriend isn't real."

Dwight slumps as if I've let the air out of his spine. "Boy, this day is starting off a real winner. It's bad luck not to name your boat, you know."

"I didn't know that, actually. I happen to know nothing about fishing or boating, so you're ahead of me there. The right name will come to you when you're ready for it." I motion to the vessel in his driveway. "It sure is beautiful. Maybe I should take up fishing. How much does a boat like that cost?"

Dwight finds his confidence once more, his chest puffing with pride. He rattles off a number that makes my eyes bulge.

"Holy cannoli! Are you serious? What kind of job in this town pays that kind of money?" It's a personal question, but I guess we're there now.

Dwight smirks at me, leaning on his doorframe. "You don't think I'm the only walking saltine cracker, do you? I make unique mascot costumes and sell them all over. I have a website, and people order whatever they need. I make them the costume and ship it to them. Anywhere all over the world."

My mouth falls open. "I had no idea the mascot business was that lucrative, or that you made your own costumes. That's really cool, Dwight."

He nods proudly. "Got a windfall of orders not too long ago. Everyone wanted to dress up as a giant heart or a big box of chocolates for Valentine's Day."

I grin at him. "That's incredible, Dwight. What a unique talent. I didn't realize you made all those costumes yourself. That's amazing."

"It is. I do that, plus I work for the school as a janitor. I live pretty simply and decided to treat myself to something grand. My dad's getting on in years. He deserves to go fishing on a real boat that we don't have to turn in at the end of the day." Dwight crosses his arms over his chest. "My dad's got Parkinson's."

For a conversation I didn't know how to start, this sure is going far deeper than I was anticipating. "Oh, gosh. I'm so sorry to hear that, Dwight. How is he feeling?"

Dwight holds his hand parallel to the floor and tilts it from side to side. "He has good days and bad ones. I want him to come out here and have such a good time that he stays. I want him to move in with me so I can look after him, but he's a Texas boy and loves it out there. I'm not sure a boat can convince him."

"Maybe just you telling him you love him will be enough." I stare at Dwight, seeing this acquaintance in a new light. "You're a good guy, Dwight."

"I try to be." He straightens, taking a step back. "Was that all you wanted? My RSVP?"

I shake my head. "That was my first of all. My second of all is that I was hoping you might be willing to come to the party in one of your costumes. It's a dress up party anyway, but the kids always have more fun when you're there."

Dwight grins at me. "I just so happen to have a giant book costume I've been looking to try out. If it moves well and holds up to the Miller boys, then I can put it on my website to sell. Do you think the librarian would like a walking, talking book to come to her birthday party?"

I clasp my hands over my heart. "I think she would be honored."

Dwight salutes me with two fingers, dismissing me from his porch so I can get to my kitchen and help Betty make the massive order of funfetti cupcakes for the party.

While I'm glad I got to know Dwight a little better, I am no closer to finding the person who stole from Jeanette and left her for dead.

14

FORGETTING TO LIVE

Betty's humming is the best sound in the world when I'm baking. Even though I know I should feel harried and hurried, her gentle voice lulls me so my hands move with more precision and fewer mistakes. While I know I have to pick up the pace, I find that I am less bothered by the enormous workload when she is near.

Of course, that could also be because she is a wiz at baking.

"I still can't believe you made all the double fudge cupcakes this morning before I got in. Why I didn't get an assistant earlier is beyond me."

Betty chortles into the mixing bowl while she adds the salt. "I'm glad to be up and moving. You know I'm no good sitting still." She makes a muscle with her bicep. "See that?

I think it's gotten firmer since I started. It's all that whipping."

I nod, making my own muscle to display proudly. "That's right. It's work plus a workout."

"With a cupcake at the end of the rainbow as a reward."

We giggle together because we are our own taste testers. It is far and away the best part of the job.

Betty blows a kiss to Buttercream as she swims in the bowl on the counter, flicking her tail at us happily. "I think we'll be finished with the cupcakes for Marianne's birthday by the end of the day today. We can frost them tomorrow."

I nod, checking our list on the fridge that we have of all the tasks that need to be done this week. It's a simple way to keep us in sync, but quite effective. "I love that the Live Forever Club is handling the actual party planning of the whole thing. I want to be more involved. I mean, Marianne is my best friend. But the orders are crazy this week." Just as they were last week, and the week before. "I'm glad you're here. Honestly, if you hadn't come along, I might be sitting in the corner of this kitchen, huddled in a ball while crying."

Betty tsks me. "We can't have that. Karen asked Rip if she could borrow the dunk tank that we keep for the summer festivals. I don't know who she plans on conning into that thing, but it's sure to be a fun day. People get crazy when there's a dunk tank."

"I'll bet. I stopped by Dwight's house this morning to

ask him if he could dress up for Marianne's party, so the kids will have that as entertainment, too."

Betty chortles. "Oh, Dwight. I've known him since he was a baby. Sweet boy."

"He seems nice. He mentioned his dad is coming to visit this week. He was excited about that."

Betty's smile falters. "Ah. Kurt doesn't stay long when he comes back to Sweetwater Falls to see his son."

"No? Does he not like it here?"

"I don't think that's it." Her voice lowers. "Kurt's wife died a good five years ago in Sweetwater Falls. She was barely in the ground before he was packed up and gone. This was their home, and he wanted nothing to do with it after she passed. I think losing her sucked the joy right out of him. Dwight stayed, taking over the mortgage for the house he grew up in, and Kurt left for Texas. Whenever he visits, I can tell it makes him sad. Too many memories of his wife."

My hands still in the bin of cupcake wrappers. "That's terrible. I had no idea. Poor Dwight."

"Poor both of them. Poor all of us. We lost Deanna, and then when Kurt couldn't bear to be here anymore, we lost him, too."

"Maybe he'll enjoy his time here with Dwight and he'll stay longer. Dwight just got that fancy fishing boat."

Betty shrugs noncommittally. "Maybe. I'm glad Dwight did something with all that money he got from his mom's life insurance policy. Kurt split it with his son, and Dwight socked it away. Smart, really. But I know it would make Deanna happy to see him using that money on something that makes her boy happy. Now that her money's going toward making memories for her husband and her son so they can go fishing together? I think that's exactly the kind of blessing she would hope might happen upon those two."

I feel horrible for suspecting Dwight of stealing Jeanette's money to buy the boat. He deserves a fun treat after all he's been through. I hope he names the boat something delightful that makes him smile.

Betty works on the batter for the next batch, and while that is mixing, she gets out the ingredients for the frosting. The woman never stops. After I showed her how to make the cupcakes, she rarely needs my help at all.

I want to do something nice for Betty, but we are still getting to know each other, so I'm not sure what that might be. But my gratitude runs high whenever she is around, because it means all the work will get done, and I won't end up a ball of nerves by the end of the day.

While I line the pans with cupcake wrappers, I watch Betty hum to herself while her hips sway. She would have made a fine ballerina; I am certain of it.

"Betty, do you ever regret going into accounting rather than being a ballerina?"

Betty chortles, wiping her hands off on her apron. "Life is too short for regrets, Charlotte. I'm sure I pouted and cried about it all when the heartbreak was fresh, but that was all so long ago. Life turned out how it was supposed to. I have no complaints." Her focus shifts to me. "How about you? This is your dream. Is it everything you hoped it would be?"

I digest her words before answering honestly. "It's more than everything I thought it would be. It's a dream come true. I just don't want it to turn into something I end up resenting. I spent so much energy making this business happen that now I worry I might only have cupcakes in my soul and little else."

Betty crosses the kitchen and pats my hand. "I think it's going to feel like that until you get used to having help. After this week, perhaps things will slow down for you, and you can go smell the flowers. Balance is the key ingredient in not resenting your dream once it comes true. We need to get you a hobby that has nothing to do with baking."

I soak in her wisdom, knowing she understands far more about life than I do in my limited knowledge of the universe. "I like that. After Marianne's party, I'll have to work some actual living into my schedule before I scale up."

Betty eyes me with a slight warning in her gaze. "Live first, then scale up. That's the order, understood? If you don't do the first one, you'll hate the second one when it comes. Anyone can build a business up; but it takes a real specific set of skills to achieve longevity. A key ingredient is to make sure you don't burn out and end up hating the thing you love."

I wince. "Oh, that would be awful. I'll do some thinking about what that might entail."

"See that you do. Don't make me sic the Live Forever Club on you. They're pretty insistent that we not gloss over the finer points in life. Like, say, living."

As I start spooning batter into the liners, Betty's advice sticks in my ribs. I'm not sure what I want out of life when it comes to fun. It seems to happen upon me rather than me seeking it out. That can't be good.

I gnaw on my lip as an idea occurs to me. While I'm sure it's insane and quite outside the box, if I'm not going to resent the business I love, then perhaps I need to start living now. To do that, I need to try new things and make life happen in unexpected ways.

"I've got to make a call. Be back in five." I abandon my cupcake batter and take my phone outside, looking up an activity that is certainly outside of my comfort zone.

I will learn to live, doggone it.

And Betty is going to be wild right alongside me.

15

BETTY'S SURPRISE

When I booked this online, I wasn't sure what I thought might happen. I do one spontaneous thing, and... what? I suddenly become a person who lives a more varied life? I become a woman who isn't one hundred percent work and no play?

As I wait outside the recreation center looking for Betty's car, I begin to regret this decision. I nearly talked myself out of showing up this morning, but Aunt Winnie wouldn't let me back out. In fact, my aunt insisted she join me in one of my few spontaneous moments, so we could experience this adventure together. I am white knuckling the steering wheel while my great-aunt applies her lipstick.

Winnie waves at Karen as she parks her golf cart in a spot.

My head whips to my great-aunt. "Did you invite Karen

and Agnes?"

Aunt Winnie shrugs. "Of course I did. I called Marianne, too. She's on her way." She reaches over and pinches my cheek. "We didn't want to miss our girl's first steps outside her box. Betty was right, you know. You don't want to be so singularly minded that you forget how to enjoy life outside your kitchen. So much of your business thrives on creativity. It matters if you try new things. Good for Betty for pushing you."

"This was supposed to be a treat for Betty. A nice surprise for her. But I figured it wouldn't hurt if I tried it, too." I wave at Marianne as she pulls up in her nice sedan, and then I walk toward the front of the building with Aunt Winnie by my side. "I really hope I don't fall on my butt in front of all of you."

"That's the thing about doing new activities with your favorite female friends. There's always someone there to pick you up when you do, inevitably, fall on your butt."

I lean my elbow on my aunt's shoulder while the women park and make their way to the front of the building. When Betty arrives, I remember why I booked this class. I wanted to do something nice for her, and something adventurous for me. It doesn't matter if I stink at this; it's a new experience.

We all take turns hugging Betty when she arrives. She turns to me, breathless from all the love she well deserves. "Okay, I'm here in sweatpants and a t-shirt, like you requested. What's all this about, Charlotte?"

I motion to the front doors. “Did you know that the high school drama teacher gives dance classes to the public on Wednesdays after school lets out?”

Betty freezes. “What?”

I smirk as she slowly puts together the pieces. “I booked us spots in her ballet class for four o’clock. I know you and I have been working all morning, so we aren’t exactly spry on our feet. But it’s now or never, right? Might as well go for it and see what we can do in there.”

Betty’s mouth drops open as she puts together my words and pairs them with the building before us. Moisture makes her eyes glassy, and when she speaks, her voice is thick with emotion. “Charlotte, you didn’t have to do this! You really booked us a ballet lesson?”

I motion to the Live Forever Club and my best friend. “All of us. We might not be ballerina material, but you were right this morning when you said that I can’t keep working while forgetting to live.”

Betty throws her arms around me, her cheeks wet with gratitude. “Oh, this is wonderful! And Winnie, you were all in on this? We’re going to have such a fun time!” She links her arms through Karen’s and Agnes’, marching us inside as if she has always been one of us.

Sometimes it’s Betty who pushes me and teaches me about life. Today, I get to give her a gentle push, marveling at her happiness as she strolls into the building to take her first ballet class in decades.

16

A BALLERINA'S WRATH

If it wasn't clear to me that I am not athletic, it is glaringly obvious by the end of the ballet lesson that I chose the correct profession in becoming a baker and not a dancer. "I think my toes fell off. Nothing that we did felt all that strenuous in the moment, but my thighs are somehow burning." I lean forward from my spot on the floor, eyeing my street shoes as if they have evil intent.

Marianne groans beside me, slumping against the wall. "Just what I needed before my birthday—to feel old. Pick up my hand and slap yourself with it. Then slap me with it if I ever let Agnes talk me into going to another ballet class. This isn't a performance. This is a full-on sport."

I chuckle at her exhaustion because it matches my own.

The high school drama teacher who acted as the ballet

instructor this afternoon goes by Madame Bartholomew. While she never raised her voice, I felt myself working harder and pushing myself to meet her even-tempered demands. She wears her silver hair pulled back in a tight bun, and her posture is picture perfect at all times. When she comes over to us as we try to fit our swollen and aching feet back into sneakers, my back instantly straightens to match hers. "Great class, Madame Bartholomew. Thanks for letting us drop in."

She nods but then locks her eyes on me. "May I speak with you a moment, Miss McKay?"

My stomach hollows as it always did when I was in school, and I knew I'd done poorly on a test. While I am certain this class is for fun and not for competitive ballerinas, I worry as I stand and follow her into the hallway that I have somehow besmirched her art with my wonky gait and ungraceful pliés. Perhaps she is about to ask me never to come back into her studio.

By the time she turns to face me in the empty hallway, I am sweating anew. "I'm sorry, Madame Bartholomew. I know I'm not a ballerina, but I wanted to try one class to see if I could do something different and expand my horizons just a little. I swear, I'll never come back and waste your valuable time like this. I really tried my hardest. I'm just no good at this sort of thing. I was born with two left feet."

Madame Bartholomew blinks at me, and then lets out

a demure chuckle at my fretting. "My, I guess I don't have to worry it was you who hurt Jeanette after all."

I blink at her before I take a step back. "I'm sorry, what? You think I hurt Jeanette? I'm the one who found Jeanette and phoned in the attack."

Madame Bartholomew folds her arms without compromising a smidgen of her posture. "I know that. But I also know that you run a bakery out of her kitchen in the back of Sweetwater Fountains. I'm sure you want more than just a kitchen. Perhaps you want a whole storefront, but Jeanette wouldn't sell the space to you. I was worried you might have grown impatient and attacked my dear friend." She shakes her head. "And right after she was yelled at in her own store."

I balk at the instructor. "Oh, wow. I mean, I guess all of that does sound a little suspect. But I would never hurt Jeanette. I adore her."

Madame Bartholomew studies my angst in the same way she sized up my nonexistent grace on the planked dance floor. She looks as if she is capable of smiling, but I see no trace of a crinkle in her features. Her petite stature does nothing to make her look less foreboding as I wait for her to measure out my innocence.

Finally, she replies. "I know Jeanette adores you. We collect rocks together by the falls every now and then. Ever since you started renting her kitchen, she worries far less about making rent. She can create now, instead of making copies of the fountains she crafted years ago."

"Jeanette has a good sense of what works," I offer, my stomach churning.

"Indeed. She uses stones she finds in Sweetwater Falls, but she also orders gems that are far more valuable than people realize. She might spend countless hours on a single fountain and crust it with more jewels than a person can measure. That girl is a treasure, and she belongs here. I want to say the same about you, but if I find that you hurt my friend, you will regret ever setting foot in this town, young lady."

I nearly vomit on the spot but manage to hold myself together. My eyes prick with moisture. "I didn't hurt Jeanette. I've been working myself ragged trying to clean up her store for her *and* keep up with my business at the same time. I care about her."

Madame Bartholomew draws herself up. "Cleaning up the storefront that you're going to move in on, now that Jeanette is in the hospital! I heard you yelling at her!"

My mouth falls open, aghast. "I've never raised my voice to Jeanette."

"You did. I was in the store, and you and Jeanette were in the backroom. I heard you yelling at her the morning she was attacked."

I gasp, scandalized. "I would never hurt someone to get ahead, and frankly, I can't manage a storefront. That's a whole other skillset that I don't have."

It's not until those words tumble out of me that I realize how very true and horrible they are. Sure, it's the dream to have a cupcakery where people can come in and order whatever they want any day of the week in any quantity—great or small. But I don't know how to run a dining area. I belong in the kitchen, not greeting people and making sure the display cases are stocked. I only hired my first employee last week, and she had to hunt me down and make me see I couldn't sustain the workload the way it was going. If Betty hadn't come into my life, I would be a sobbing mess, instead of able to take time for the occasional ballet class after work.

My hand goes over my mouth, as if that will shove my insecurities back inside of me where they've been lurking and rotting while people praise my business for growing at the rate it has.

I don't know what I'm doing.

I back up, stunned at the revelation that no doubt everyone saw coming except for me.

I rush out of the building, leaving Madame Bartholomew to keep her poor opinion of me. My own opinion of myself is just as low.

17

OVERWHELMED

I've been trying to avoid Marianne because I'm afraid I'll say something to spoil her surprise birthday party. But after being confronted by Madame Bartholomew for a crime I didn't commit, I am restless.

The next day, I bake several hundred cupcakes by myself, since it's Betty's day off. The moment I finish for the day, I beeline straight to the library on the edge of panic. Marianne is just about to close for the evening, and I catch her as the last person leaves with a stack of books in their arms.

Marianne brightens when she sees me, but then springs toward me when she sees my unhappiness plain on my face. "Oh, Charlotte! What happened?"

I throw my arms around my best friend, shocked that I thought I could last a whole day without a hug from her.

Marianne is petite, and folds easily into my arms. "Madame Bartholomew thinks I got in a yelling match with Jeanette the day of her accident. After the class yesterday, she accused me of putting Jeanette in the hospital! She thinks I want to shut down Sweetwater Fountains so I can open a storefront for the bakery. After all Jeanette's done for me, how could Madame Bartholomew think I would stoop so low?"

Marianne pulls back, tugging a tissue from her pocket in case I should burst into tears, which I hope doesn't happen. "You know none of that is true. Madame Bartholomew has a stick up her butt. Always has. She rarely takes a shine to anyone, and when she finally does, no one is good enough for her very small handful of approved friends. It's not you; this is all par for the course with her."

I shake my head. "The things she said. I almost believed her!"

"That's silly. You're getting all upset about someone's opinion who's got a negative thing to say about practically everyone she meets. Don't waste your tears on her approval. Because trust me, it'll do you no good." She shakes her head at me. "Why didn't you tell me about this yesterday when it happened?"

"I was too embarrassed. I didn't want you to think I could ever hurt Jeanette!"

"Oh, Charlotte," Marianne hugs me again, squeezing

until the angry ballet instructor's words begin to fade. Marianne's kindness is exactly what my heart needs to finally find its way to calm.

"I'm tired," I admit. "It's been so good to have Betty working as my assistant. She's fantastic and I really need the help. But I miss you. We can't go this many days in a week without seeing each other. I don't have it in me!"

Marianne holds me tighter. "Agreed! I feel the same way, even though we just saw each other yesterday. But it wasn't long enough, and we've had too many gaps in between. Someone came in today and asked for help finding a baking cookbook. I couldn't help but think how ordinary those recipes in the book were and how brilliant yours are. I miss getting all sugared up and messy in your kitchen."

When we finally release each other, Marianne leads me over to the circulation desk, hopping up on the counter since it's just the two of us. "I know this is silly, but it's my birthday this weekend. I never make a big deal out of birthdays, but this one feels big. Could we do something, just the two of us?"

I nod, grateful I have a way to get her to the surprise party organically. "Absolutely. I'll plan the whole thing. You just show up in your birthday best. Sunday? Maybe three o'clock?"

Marianne's feet dangle, her heels hitting the wood. "Perfect. I want time with my best friend on my special day."

"Done. Don't think on it another second."

Marianne points at the bags under my eyes. "Then you don't get to obsess about Madame Bartholomew's approval. We'll figure out who was yelling at Jeanette one way or another."

I pinch the bridge of my nose after I hop up on the counter beside her. "The thing is, a lot of the stuff she said about me wanting Jeanette out of the picture so I could have the whole space for my business got me thinking. I don't know how I would even dream of expanding the bakery. I don't know how to run a storefront. I don't have the first clue how the managerial part of the gig even works. I wasn't even thinking about expanding until Madame Bartholomew said all that, and then I realized that it's not in the cards for me. It's ridiculous, because I don't need a storefront. The business is going just fine. But to know my business' limitations are my fault? I can't expand because I don't know how to run a store? It's depressing."

Marianne taps her littlest finger to mine. "Hey, you didn't know how to run a bakery out of the kitchen, and you learned. Lisa taught you and you followed the instructions. This is no different. You just need a teacher, if this is what you want." She touches the outside of her shoe to mine. "Is that what you want?"

"I don't know!" I fret, losing my cool all over again. "I have no idea what I want. All I know is that I wasn't freaking out about expanding into a storefront until yesterday, and now I'm doomed because if it's up to me to figure this out and do it correctly, we're screwed!"

Of all things, Marianne chuckles. "You're not screwed. My goodness, Charlotte. How stressful it must be inside that head of yours. There's no way any person knows the ins and outs of a business they've never run before. How do you think people learn?"

I shrug. "They just have the knack for business." I motion to my head. "I've got cupcakes only up in here."

Marianne snickers at me. "They learned, just as you will learn, if that's what you want. How about you tackle one giant headache at a time. You just hired your first employee. That's a big victory! Maybe sit with that for a while and get the hang of it. When you want to think about expanding, the education will be there for you."

I rest the side of my head to hers. "You think?" I can feel a portion of my stress deflating, the knot in my chest loosening ever so slightly.

"I *know*. I'll even help you find it. There's nothing the two of us can't do if we put our minds to it. This is a panic attack for another day, Charlotte. For now, get the hang of having an employee and doing payroll. Those are big deal skills you'll need if you're going to expand someday. You're already stacking building blocks without even realizing it. You've got this." She links her arm through mine. "And I've got you."

Relief sweeps over me when Marianne's words start to

sneak past my anxiety, quelling it the longer I digest her wisdom.

"I don't have to know everything right now. I just have to do what I'm doing, and when I feel like expanding, you'll help me figure out how?"

Marianne smiles at me. "Absolutely. By then, this whole mess with Madame Bartholomew will be over." She whirls around and hops behind the desk, plucking her phone from her purse. "I'm so in your corner that I'm going to wrap up this Madame Bartholomew mess, too."

My neck shrinks at how childish I've been. "You don't have to do that."

Marianne holds up her hand to silence me as her call connects. "Madame Bartholomew? This is Marianne. Yes, the librarian. What business do you have making Charlotte McKay upset like this?"

I bury my face in my hands, utterly ashamed that I fell apart so easily. I should have thicker skin.

I should also be working less and sleeping more.

Marianne's hip juts to the side. She's a mouse when it comes to speaking up for herself, but for me, she's a linebacker with an attitude. "And when did you hear them arguing?" She pauses and then scoffs. "I was with Charlotte at that time. We were in the kitchen, music playing, so she's got an alibi. The next time you want to bully someone, perhaps dig a little deeper instead of picking a person at random to crush." Another pause, and Marianne's nose crinkles. "What bracelet?" She holds the phone from her face. "Charlotte, did you buy a bracelet from the store?"

I hold up my wrist. "Jeanette gave me a bracelet a couple months back when we first met."

"You hear that? It was a gift. Just because the person yelling at Jeanette said she bought a bracelet that day doesn't mean that the nearest person to you wearing a bracelet is guilty of attempted murder and robbery."

Another pause. "No, Charlotte didn't pay for the bracelet. Do you pay for gifts?"

Marianne harrumphs and then ends the call before shoving her phone back into her purse. "The nerve of some people!"

I give her a slow clap. "That was incredible! You didn't have to do that. I got all worked up when I should have had perspective. I let myself get all turned around."

Marianne's lips purse before she speaks. "Jeanette and some woman were yelling, according to Madame Bartholomew. The woman bought a bracelet that day, and was mad that it didn't bring her luck, as the stones were supposed to. She came back and was yelling at Jeanette about it." Marianne loops her purse over her shoulder, then slowly meets my gaze. "Charlotte, if the woman bought a bracelet the day of the attack..."

I perk up, leaping off the counter with renewed pep. "Then there would be a copy of the receipt, complete with card information and the name if she didn't pay in cash!"

While I was exhausted and scattered just minutes ago, now I feel renewed with purpose. We are going to get to the bottom of who hurt Jeanette, hopefully tonight.

18

GUILTY GIRLS

After racing to Sweetwater Fountains only to find that Jeanette's register and receipts had been confiscated by the police, Marianne and I decided to head home and call the precinct when it opened in the morning. While I couldn't get ahold of Logan, I spoke with another officer who took down the information and promised to talk to the sheriff about it first thing in the morning.

While I want to see the receipt for myself, for now, that will have to do.

Besides, after yet another restless night of sleep, I have a long day of baking ahead of me. I need to keep my head in the game if I'm going to get things done in time.

I beat Betty to the bakery, which was the plan. She's not scheduled to come in for another hour, so I have the place to myself. Friday mornings are insane with orders, and I have to frost several dozen cupcakes still before I can start boxing them for pickup.

The swirls are rushed but still pretty, the frosting standing up and making each cupcake look like the perfect treat.

I go as fast as I can without chancing a sacrifice in quality. It's hard to get the count right, and I start second-guessing myself as the orders begin to blur in my mind. Several times, I have to start over on an order, recounting the flavors because I put an assortment instead of the dozen double fudge that they requested.

I massage my temples as I step back from the rows and rows of pink boxes, all squawking to be filled.

My bracelet from Jeanette dangles on my wrist, so I rub the stones. She told me the green gems were for serenity, which I desperately now need. I don't know if this sort of thing actually works, but the motion of rubbing the smooth stones sooths me enough to get my mind back on track.

"Thanks, Jeanette," I say aloud to the hollow of the kitchen.

When I refocus in on the order I am filling, my mind clears itself of the clutter so I can get myself together without too many blunders.

I would attribute it to the type of stones on my bracelet, but part of me is sure that no matter what color they were, I would have found a slice of sanity by simply believing clarity was possible and taking a moment to breathe.

I always forget that breathing part.

I can't believe that someone would yell at Jeanette because they expected instantaneous luck from the purchase of a bracelet, but it didn't come to fruition. I can't imagine the kind of person who would do that.

Then again, I'm guessing if that is the same person who attacked Jeanette, they aren't operating with all their marbles.

When Betty arrives, she takes over making more funfetti cupcakes for Marianne's party while I hand out the orders to the people who show up at nine sharp. Each person gives me an excited smile and tells me which character they are going to get dressed as for Marianne's surprise party. Betty watches the process, and takes over for me whenever I need a break. She offers another cheery face to brighten my customers' morning.

To my credit, I only flubbed two orders, giving them the wrong kind of cupcakes, which I was happy to fix.

When the last box is delivered, I sag against the closed door, slumping to the floor.

"You did it!" Betty cheers for me, a piping bag in her hand. "I don't know how you did all this without an assistant. Not to toot my own horn, but you need me for big orders like this."

I nod without a hint of ire. "Absolutely. I would have had to pull an all-nighter. Several, no doubt."

Betty keeps her head down while she frosts. "You've been too busy for me to thank you properly for the ballet lesson. And the fact that you invited the Live Forever Club? That was such a treat. Thank you, Charlotte. You're the best boss I've ever had."

I chuckle from my spot on the floor. I have chocolate stains on my apron and something sticky on my forehead, so I definitely don't feel like the best boss in the world when that is coupled with my exhaustion, but I'll take the compliment all the same. "You were a graceful ballerina, for sure."

Betty keeps her chin down. "You ran out of there before I could say thank you. Madame Bartholomew caught me on the way out. She had a few words to say, that's for sure."

My stomach tightens. "A few words to say about how I'm the thief?"

Betty's jaw firms as she keeps her eyes on her work. "Actually, she accused *me* of being the thief. I saw the two of you talking in the hallway, so I'm guessing she had something to say about me to you. I just wanted to clear the air and tell you that I didn't hurt Jeanette. I came to the shop afterhours to help clean it up, not to steal her merchandise."

My jaw drops, but Betty continues before I can speak.

"Though, I suppose Madame Bartholomew has compelling evidence against me. She pointed out that any person applying to make cupcakes all day must have an ulterior motive. She thinks the best way for me to steal more from Jeanette would be to work for you, where I have unfettered access to Sweetwater Fountains.

It sounds logical when she laid it all out like that, but I had nothing to do with the break-in. I really do want to spend my retirement baking cupcakes. I like it in here. We can sing and dance and be silly together. I've been sitting behind a desk for decades. I've been dying to dance."

I pull myself to my feet, crossing the space between us so I can get in Betty's eyeline. "I know you didn't start working here so you could get easy access to Sweetwater Fountains. That much is obvious. We've been cleaning up her store together and not once have you pocketed anything."

"I really haven't."

I gently take the piping bag from Betty's hand. "I know that. Madame Bartholomew did stop me after the class yesterday, but it wasn't to talk about you. She accused me of the same thing. Said I wanted to expand my cupcakery into Jeanette's storefront, which I have no plans to do."

Betty tilts her chin up, gaping at me. "Do you know how much sleep I lost last night? I was mortified that my character might ever come into question! Why, if I didn't have the best day of dancing in my entire life yesterday, I would go over there and show her what a dangerous criminal really looks like. Unbelievable." She motions to me. "I know you didn't hurt Jeanette. You've been cleaning up her store for her!"

I hold my hands out to Betty. "Same thing can be said about you!"

She crinkles her nose. "You called in the crime! Why would you squeal on yourself?"

I shrug, relieved that Betty isn't nervous to be working with me. "Right?" We share an elated chuckle, shaking our heads at the irony of it all. "Neither of us hurt Jeanette or robbed her store, but Marianne and I might have a lead on who did. I called it in this morning to the police. Here's hoping it's all worked out by now, and they've tracked down the culprit."

I explain to Betty the altercation involving a bracelet that didn't bring enough luck to its buyer.

Betty raises her wrist guiltily. "I bought this from Jeanette last year. I don't have the receipt, but it's from Sweetwater Fountains! Do you think this counts as evidence?"

I shake my head. "No. I have one, too. It only means we have good taste, not that we're thieves." I hand her back her piping bag. "Did your bracelet bring you luck?"

"Not if I get thrown in jail for a crime I didn't commit." Betty sighs. "Mine isn't supposed to bring me luck. It brings me love, which I have in spades. Rip is a fantastic husband."

"Mine brings me serenity," I inform her.

Betty chortles. "You might want to look in a mirror. You've got frosting in your hair, dear. Perhaps you should recharge those gemstones, or however that works. You could use an extra dose of serenity these days."

"You are not wrong." I squeeze Betty, grateful to have

done the Friday morning rush with a friend by my side. "You're my serenity," I tell her. "Without you, I would have more problems than just frosting in my hair. I would be pulling *out* my hair!"

Betty chuckles, patting my back before I release her. "Glad to help." She shakes her head. "Look at the two of us, thieves and bakers."

I tsk us both as I move toward the refrigerator. "Someone's got to keep us in line."

Though, as I say this, I wonder if there will be a time when Jeanette comes back because her attacker has been brought to justice.

Surely the culprit's good luck bracelet will run out soon.

19

DWIGHT'S DISTRACTION

I have never seen so much of Dwight in my life as I have this week. Not that I'm complaining, but he's quite the presence when he's around.

"I've never had a funfetti cupcake before. Can't wait to try it. How many sprinkles do you think you go through in a week, Charlotte?"

I don't remember the steps that led me to tell Dwight he could come into my kitchen while I worked so he could talk my ear off, but it's happening, and there's no going back now. "I'm really not sure, Dwight."

He seems to have very little understanding of body language, which I am communicating with in spades. My back is to him while I sift my dry ingredients. I've been barely speaking while Dwight regales me with stories of all the birthday cakes he has ever tasted, and then proceeds to rank them best to worst.

I regret going to his house to poke around and see if he might be guilty of stealing from Jeanette's register. Now, apparently, we're best friends.

Excellent.

It's Betty's day off, so it's just Dwight and me in my kitchen. He's sitting in the sole chair and I'm working my butt off, trying to find a polite way to ask him to leave.

He motions around my kitchen. "Business seems to be going well for you. I mean, you're renting a commercial kitchen. I love it when a local business thrives. If I don't have to leave Sweetwater Falls to buy something, so much the better. The more things we can get locally, I'm satisfied."

"Uh-huh." Dwight prattles on about the various businesses that have existed here throughout the years until I finally interject with a breathy, "Wow. It's nearly noon, Dwight. Do you think you might be going home to work on your costumes now?"

It's the most direct I can be without shoving him out the door.

"No, I'm waiting on the glue to dry on a few pieces, then I can do some of the larger assembly. It all goes in stages. See, when I start a costume, I can see it in 3-D down to the studs. Not literal studs, mind you. But I can see the whole project from beginning to end."

I close my eyes, praying for patience while I cream the wet ingredients.

When Aunt Winnie stops by with a sandwich for me, I

nearly bowl her over with a hug. "Take Dwight out!" I beg her in a whisper.

Aunt Winnie chuckles. "He won't leave, eh?"

I pull back, eyes wide to convey my exasperation.

She chucks my shoulder in a "buck up" sort of way. "Looks like it's time to find your big girl voice and speak up for yourself." Then she increases her volume and waves to Dwight. "Hi, there. Is Charlotte teaching you how to bake?"

Dwight shakes his head. "Actually, I was about to take her through the steps of how I make my costumes. It's more detailed than people realize."

I shoot Aunt Winnie a look of sheer desperation, but she merely grins in reply. She nods along to Dwight's monologue, dips her finger in a bowl of frosting and pops it in her mouth, then she kisses my cheek on her way out, not bothering to say goodbye to Dwight, who has started his explanation of how to make a giant book mascot costume all over again.

I do not want to learn this life lesson. I don't want to dip into awkwardness and tell Dwight to please go away. I want to be a nice person, but I think I am becoming more of a pushover than anything else.

My shoulders slump as I drag my feet back to my mixing bowl, glancing up at my goldfish in silent supplication for her to do the dirty work of telling Dwight to scram.

It's when Carlos comes by an hour later that I nearly snap.

"Hey, Dwight. This is Carlos, Marianne's boyfriend. We need to have a serious conversation about law stuff, so I'll have to cut our time together short. We were just about to go for a walk."

Dwight's head bobs as he waves me off. "Go on. I'll hold down the fort while you're gone."

I fight back a silent scream as I take off my apron and motion for Carlos to come and get some fresh air with me. As soon as we get a healthy distance from the bakery, I jab my finger at Carlos. "When we get back, you're doing the dirty work of making sure Dwight leaves with you. He's been hanging around the kitchen all morning, and I'm reaching my breaking point."

"He won't leave?"

"No!"

"What did he say when you asked him to go home?"

I glower at Carlos. "Look, you. I don't have it in me to tell someone to get lost. I'm not assertive in that authoritative way. So, you have to do it. I can't. I'm physically incapable."

Carlos chuckles at me. "Wow. That's some limitation you've got there. How do you get anything done?"

"I've got an excellent system of grinding my teeth while I silently stew."

Carlos gives birth to a full-bellied laugh. "I'll get rid of him for you. I stopped by to see if you needed any help with the party. The Live Forever Club said they had everything handled, but I don't want to do nothing. Marianne deserves a full team effort."

My mouth pulls to the side while I think. "I could use help getting all the cupcakes to the library. They're mostly all packaged up and sitting in my fridge right now. I was planning on making a few trips, but I could use a second car to make things go quicker. I'm supposed to be taking Marianne out, being her diversion so I get her there at the right time, so the surprise is pulled off. Maybe you could help Agnes with the food after you help me with the cupcake drop-off?"

"Agnes says she's got that covered. Karen's in charge of coordinating the petting zoo company. Winifred is handling beverages and decorations. I'm useless." He gives me an exaggerated frown, shoving his hands into the pockets of his khaki pants.

"Aunt Winnie will need help hanging the decorations, for sure. I'm supposed to lend a hand that morning, but I'm going to be cutting it close. Could I pass that job off to you?"

Carlos nods, relieved to be useful. "Absolutely. Thank you."

"Which storybook character are you going as?" I ask conversationally, impressed that I still remember how to make pleasant small talk after working by myself all morning with Dwight talking at me.

"I can't tell you."

I quirk an eyebrow at him. "The Invisible Man?"

Carlos smirks. "No. But it would ruin the surprise. You'll just have to wait and see. How about you?"

I grimace. "Gosh, I really should be thinking about that, shouldn't I." I bat my hand at the problem, as if that will make it go away. "Something will come to me."

Carlos and I walk in the chilly sunshine, talking about how things are going in his new office, which cases he's most excited to work on, and which cases are proving problematic.

I don't often get to spend time with just Carlos, so we take the scenic stroll until we reach a store I have yet to peruse.

He opens the door for me, ushering me through. "I was hoping you could help me pick out Marianne's birthday gift. It's my first birthday with her, so I want it to be nice."

I glance around at the sparkly jewelry begging for fancy ladies to try everything on to see how each piece shines. I gape at Carlos as I whirl on him. "We're in a jewelry store! Are you proposing?" I don't mean to shout, but it comes out an accusation.

He holds up his hands with a smile. "No. Someday, but not today. I thought I would pick your brain to see what kind of bracelet or necklace you think she would like."

My hand flies over my heart. "That is the absolute sweetest. I'm sure she'll love anything you pick out."

"Stop telling me what I want to hear and help me!" Carlos looks at the jewelry cases as if everything is written in a language he has no hope of understanding. "She deserves the best, and I have no idea how to pick that out, other than getting the most expensive item, which doesn't seem like the kind of thing Marianne would care about."

I shake my head. "Jewelry is always nice, Carlos. Think about who Marianne is. Her day-to-day. The colors and things she wears."

Carlos closes his eyes as if meditating might conjure a pathway to the perfect gift.

I do the same, worried that I haven't landed on a present for my best friend, either. I've been so focused on the cupcakes that I haven't even ventured into a store to purchase something she would enjoy unwrapping.

I think about my best friend and all the joy she has brought to my life. My mind begins to compile a short list of activities she does, even if they seem unimportant in the moment.

Marianne loves to read, obviously, but she has unfettered access to any book she could ever want.

She knits, but not passionately enough to have a bin of yarn. She just picks up the items for making one specific thing. She doesn't feel the need to stockpile without a plan.

No, buying her more yarn wouldn't be helpful.

I chew on my lower lip, wondering what sort of gift might tell her "I love you" and also "I see you."

Because at the end of the day, a woman wants to be seen and loved by the people she chooses to keep in her life.

It's then that an idea settles in my brain. My eyes open

in time with Carlos', both of us sharing an excited grin. "I know what to get her!" we say together.

And what we have in mind isn't for sale in a jewelry store.

Carlos and I talk animatedly about how my gift and his go perfectly together, and that she should open his first, and then mine so she can get the full impact.

By the time we get back to my kitchen, Dwight's car is mercifully gone. "I did it!" I exclaim to Carlos. "I got Dwight to leave! I didn't realize the trick was to remove myself from the premises."

"Take away the audience, and the performer has no reason to put on a show."

Carlos' sage wisdom makes me chuckle as I move into the kitchen.

I stop short at the sight the greets me.

"Holy..." Carlos breathes, his eyes wide at the sight. He pulls out his phone, doing what a person should do when their business has been ransacked.

My chest heaves with a mix of shock and fear.

I was gone half an hour, and in that time, someone broke into my business and trashed the place, searching for who knows what.

Whatever they took, they stole my sanity, too.

20

BROKEN DREAMS

While I don't often hide myself away like a child, sitting on the floor of the pantry with the door closed and the lights off seems like the thing to do when one's business has just been broken into.

I pull my knees to my chest, my quavering chin resting atop them while fat tears roll down my cheeks.

This is my happy place. This is my business. This is my dream come true.

And now it's an utter mess.

Sometimes I can make a plan in the face of disaster or uncertainty, but today is not that day. I can't even bring myself to look at the chaos; so broken is my heart that someone would stoop this low.

At least they didn't empty the fridge of Marianne's birthday cupcakes, which seems to be the only upside to this whole ordeal.

"What were they even searching for?" I hear someone say outside the closed pantry door. "It's all baking ingredients and kitchen equipment. Marianne, can you take inventory of everything? We need to see what all's been stolen."

Despite their many attempts to lure me out of the pantry, I refuse to move. I even go so far as to lock the door from the inside so they can't get me out.

I don't care that I am behaving like a child. All I want is to be left alone, in hopes that will make the horror I saw undo itself in my mind.

My commercial mixer is on the floor with batter spilled on the silver concrete. The sugar bin has been tipped over, as if I might be hiding something of value in the granules. The cupboards were opened and emptied, with the contents on the floor and counters. Whatever they were looking for, I don't know if they found it, or what it could possibly be.

I bake cupcakes. That's all that's going on here. I can't believe anyone would want to take anything from my business, or from me.

I bury my face in my knees, clutching my body tight because I feel as if I might shatter apart if I don't physically hold myself together.

It is a long time of police and friends coming in and out of my cupcakery before Marianne uses her key to unlock the pantry, forcing her way into the space on tiptoe. "Charlotte? Oh, honey. Why are you sitting in the dark?"

I keep my face buried in my knees. "I don't want to see it all destroyed."

Marianne sits in front of me, and even though I can't see her because I have my head down, I feel her presence and the tranquility she brings to every circumstance.

Marianne runs her fingers through my mess of strawberry blonde curls. "I took inventory of all the small appliances. Anything that might be valuable and hard to replace. It's all still here. No one took anything. It seems like they were looking for something and couldn't find it. Nothing is broken, Charlotte." She grimaces. "Well, the whisk for the commercial mixer was bent, but Carlos twisted it back into shape."

That should cheer me up, and it probably does, but I can't feel much beyond my shock and grief right now.

Marianne tries again. "It looks like the door was unlocked, because there's no signs of forced entry. Logan's partner, Wayne, is going to Dwight's home to question him, since Carlos mentioned you two left him here by himself. Maybe he saw something that can shed some light on the whole thing." Marianne rests her hand on mine. "Did you and Dwight have a fight? Is there any reason you can think that he might be the one to have done this?"

That is the only thing that can raise my chin. "What?"

"Dwight. He was here while you were out. Did you two have a disagreement? Any reason to think he might be responsible for trashing the place?"

My face pulls as I consider the odd suggestion. "I

would be very surprised if he did all that. Dwight was telling me about how he makes mascot costumes. In detail. Hours of him telling me every step of how a costume comes to be. There was no argument. I barely spoke a word."

Marianne's lips purse as she pulls a tissue from her pocket and dabs at my cheeks. "Right now, Dwight is the only suspect. Is there anyone else who might have it out for you?"

I swallow, trying to guess at who might despise me enough to ransack my business. "Madame Bartholomew hates my guts, but I doubt she would do something like this." I swipe at my cheeks. "I have no idea."

Marianne scoots beside me, her arms encircling my form so I can cry on her shoulder. "Good thing all your orders are online. There's no cash to take from the bakery in a break-in."

I sniffle, blinking my tears out of the way. "Do you think that's what they were looking for? Petty cash?"

Marianne shrugs. "It's the most logical reason for a break-in."

I shake my head. "Did they break into Sweetwater Fountains via the kitchen? Is Jeanette's office a mess again?" I groan into my hands. "Is there more I'm going to be cleaning up?"

Logan's voice greets me from the doorway. "I'm going to need you to look at the office to see if it's different than how you last left it. I know you've been cleaning it up for Jeanette."

Marianne pulls me to my feet when my body doesn't seem to be able to move on its own. She hands me to Logan, whose arm curves around me. He shields my eyes with his hand like a visor, limiting my vision so I don't have to see the devastation that imprints itself in my brain every time I blink. "I'll get this all cleaned up," Logan assures me in his non-work voice. Though he needs to be on the job right now, he still softens himself for me.

Logan walks me to the door that leads to the back hallway of Sweetwater Fountains. The room on the other side is Jeanette's office, which is not how I last left it.

My hand flies over my mouth. "Oh, no! Betty and I worked so hard to get this all sorted for Jeanette!"

Logan's shoulders sink as he talks into his comm, telling his coworkers that the span of the break-in includes Jeanette's office.

The stacks of papers that Betty and I sorted the other day so Jeanette wouldn't come back to a disorganized mess are all over the place.

The storefront is much the same. My stomach feels hollow when I observe the scope of the damage. There are more items broken. More sales racks tipped over.

More work for Betty and myself to shoulder.

With a shaking hand, I point out the newly acquired damage.

Marianne marvels at the mess. "I can't believe they did all this in less than half an hour."

Logan frowns. "What did they want? Why hit the same place twice? And why bring the cupcakery into the mix? What's missing? Anything?"

It's then that my gaze beelines to the one valuable I know is worth more than the rest. "The fancy fountain!"

"Which one?" Marianne follows me as I cross the room, suddenly focused.

My eyes close as I run my hand over the fountain that was left untouched during the first break-in. "It was too heavy to move. Of course they would come back with a tool to remove the gemstones."

I touch the cavities where the large gems were inlaid. "They were here. Real gemstones that were worth more than the others." I close my eyes, resting my forehead on the lip of the sparkly concrete fountain that is as tall as I am. "It was a robbery all along. Nothing more complicated than greed. They took the cash and anything easy to grab on the first run, and then came back for the valuable gems on the second go." I purse my lips before the next thought pops into my mind. "Jeanette was just at the wrong place at the wrong time. It was random, not premeditated."

Marianne tilts her head to the side. "How can you judge that? If anything, I think it was absolutely premeditated. They went for the one fountain with real gems in it. They had to have been in here before, to have known this was the one to hit."

I shrug, knowing that both sides could be argued just fine. “I have no idea. All I know is that Jeanette’s been robbed again, my kitchen is trashed, and I have no idea who could have done something so horrible.”

Marianne curves her arm around me, guiding me out of Sweetwater Fountains and into the sunshine, where hopefully nothing so terrible has ever happened.

21

LOVE AND SUPPORT

The urge to take a nap is strong. All I want is to sleep away the day in hopes that might make it all disappear.

No such luck. After talking with Logan's dad at the station, telling him what little I've learned while Carlos corroborates my story, I know I have to head back to the Bravery Bakery to do what needs to be done. I have nearly a hundred orders left to fill, because so many cupcakes were smashed and toppled to the floor. Not to mention the birthday cupcakes that still need to be frosted. At least those weren't messed with, since I had them stored in the fridge.

It's been nearly three hours since I discovered the disaster, but when I return, a miracle has happened.

"What on earth?" My jaw hangs open, marveling at

what simply cannot be. I scrub my eyes, surveying every inch that has been cleaned to perfection. "How did…"

But the answer to the question I can't seem to work out appears from the hallway, meandering into the store with an armful of pans.

"Aunt Winnie?" Surprise hits me as my brain fights to make sense of the sight. "You didn't clean this. There's no way."

Aunt Winnie sets the cupcake pans in my sink, fixing me with a stern look. "I'll have you know that I am very much capable of cleaning a kitchen. I've cleaned more kitchens than you've baked cupcakes."

I hold up my hands. "I have no doubt. But this place was a disaster! How did you do this? Was I gone longer than I thought? Like, three days instead of three hours?"

Agnes barrels in after my great-aunt with a broom and dustpan in her grip. "Oh, come off it, Winnie. You had help."

Aunt Winnie raises her chin sanctimoniously. "Sure, but I could have done it all myself."

Karen comes in behind the two, brushing her dainty hands on her slacks. "I daresay we make a great team. First project: clean a kitchen after a heist. Second project: perform our own heist where someone else gets to clean up the mess."

"Third project: world domination?" Agnes suggests with a grin rounding her jaw.

Karen taps her nose. "Absolutely."

My hand covers my mouth as astonishment hits me hard. "You cleaned my kitchen for me. This whole sight was absolutely awful. I was dreading coming back to it. But you went ahead and fixed the nightmare." I trip forward and wrap my arms around the Live Forever Club. "Thank you. I don't know what I would do without you."

"Crash and burn," Karen supplies. "That's what we bring to the table. Lifesaving solace."

"And sweet tea!" Agnes chimes in, dumping the rest of the pans into the sink to be washed later. If all I have to do is wash the pans, I'm getting off easy.

I can't believe how lucky I am to have a team of amazing women who support and love me enough to put elbow grease behind their affection for me. Not many are this fortunate.

And that's when it hits me that even though there are plenty of reasons to be upset, because I have real love and support, I just might be the luckiest of girls.

Jeanette wasn't quite so lucky, because Betty and I have to start over, cleaning up her storefront.

I wave off the offer of sweet tea, grabbing up the broom and dustpan. "Actually, since you lovely ladies cleaned up my store, I now have the time to help tidy up Jeanette's place. She doesn't deserve to have to see her life's dream shattered. I can speak from experience now that it's the worst."

Winifred, Agnes and Karen exchange bolstering looks, and then nod as one. "We're in."

"I didn't mean for you to have to do it, too! You've done enough. Really."

It's as if I haven't spoken. They grab up rags, a mop and cleaning solution, along with the large garbage bin. Everything is dragged into Sweetwater Fountains, where the four of us clean for the next two hours.

No, I'm not on my own in this life, and neither is Jeanette.

22

PROUD PAPA

I don't feel good that Dwight is being questioned, seeing as he was left alone in my bakery before the break-in. If I had just been more direct, he wouldn't be in this situation. Is he a little irritating? Sure. Is he my favorite person in Sweetwater Falls? Not exactly. However, he's not responsible for the robbery; I'm sure of it. The only thing he's guilty of is not being able to take a hint.

I feel like a cupcake is the thing to bring in these sorts of situations to break the ice and let him know that I didn't tell the police he was the culprit.

But when the door to Dwight's home opens the morning of Marianne's surprise party, it's not the quirky, unaware man I spent far too many hours with the day before. "Hi, I'm looking for Dwight?" I say to the man in his sixties.

The man perks up. "Are you my Dwight's girlfriend? It's so nice to meet you!"

I grimace—probably rudely—and immediately fight to rectify the misunderstanding. "No! No, sir. I'm Charlotte McKay. I didn't realize Dwight had a girlfriend, but it's not me."

He shakes my hand as if he means to take it off and put it in his sweater pocket. I can feel the slight tremor in his grip, and wonder if this is Dwight's father, whom I've learned has Parkinson's.

"Oh, my mistake," he says with a cheery grin. "Glad to meet you. I'm Kurt. I just got here last night. The town hasn't changed much since I left a few decades ago." He motions to himself. "Decades! Can you believe it? I'm aging before your very eyes, but I still feel like a spring chicken. We've got good genetics, I tell you. My Dwight is the best this town has to offer. He's an entrepreneur, did you know that?"

I open my mouth because it seems like this is the part where I should respond with an affirmative grunt or something, but my input, however small, would just slow Kurt down.

"Did you know that this street used to have bushes on the end of the crosswalk just there? Can you imagine? Bushes up to your eyebrows. There's nothing I like better than a pop of nature everywhere you look. Do you like the great outdoors? I live in Texas now, and let me tell you, it's not as green as it is here. Browner, which is mighty fine most of the time, but I forget what a time capsule this place is. Absolutely stunning. Have you lived here long? I don't recall anyone having a daughter named Charlotte. At least, not when I lived here."

Again, I keep thinking that he means to leave space for me to reply, but he plows through unencumbered.

"I can't believe how long it's been since I've visited my boy. Of course, he's not a little boy anymore. He's a grown man with a business and everything. You sure you're not his girlfriend?"

I open my mouth, but again, it's unnecessary for me to speak.

"My Dwight is a catch, I tell you. There's no one better in the whole town. He could be famous with his costume making, but he keeps himself hidden away here. Thank goodness for the internet, am I right?"

I catch of glimpse of Dwight, shaking his hands as he emerges from what I'm guessing is the bathroom behind his father. "Dwight!" I flag him down, desperate not to be rude, but also not to be held hostage in this non-conversation a moment longer. "Dwight, I brought you a cupcake!"

Dwight's brows raise as he ambles toward me, standing beside his father. "Hey, Cupcake Queen. Didn't get enough drama yesterday? Back for more?"

I take the tiny margin of breath and push my point before his father can suck all the air out of the atmosphere. "Dwight, I stopped by to tell you I'm sorry that they brought you in for questioning. I know you didn't trash my business. I'm so sorry it blew back on you." I shove the small pink box into his arms. "I brought you a cupcake to apologize."

Dwight pops open the lid, grinning at the sprinkled treat. "I was hoping you would have an extra I could preview before the party today."

Kurt runs his hands over the front of his shirt. "I knew my boy had a thriving social life. Hit of the party!" He elbows his son. "See? Apple doesn't fall far from the tree. Can you see where my son gets his good looks?"

I don't know how to comment on that, because Dwight has never struck me as particularly handsome.

I mean, he looks nothing like Logan.

As if Logan can sense when I am thinking about him, my phone chimes in my pocket with a text from my boyfriend. Instead of standing there while Kurt tells me the story of how alike the two of them are, based on their respective first days of kindergarten, which apparently, I "wouldn't believe how identical they are," I wave goodbye with an apologetic tilt of my head as I back away, pressing the phone to my cheek. "You have excellent timing, Logan. What's up?"

He chuckles, but I can tell his heart isn't invested in joy. "One of my many notable virtues, I'm sure. I was just calling to check on you after everything that went down yesterday. Winnie told me the Live Forever Club cleaned up your bakery. There was nothing for me to do to help out. Can I take you out to lunch to help clear your head?"

I shove my keys into my ignition and drive away from Dwight's home before I can get sucked into part two of ten million of Kurt's stories. "I would take you up on that, but I'm running behind on all I have to do for Marianne's party."

"Did you remember that Carlos is helping you drive the cupcakes over this afternoon? I told him I could help, too, so you don't have to worry about it."

"That would be so helpful. But I have to actually package them up if we're going to transport them. They're all lined up on the counter right now, because I had to frost them this morning. Took a quick break from that, but I'll be to the bakery soon to finish that job. Might want them to make it there in one piece, rather than a pile of crumbs and frosting."

"Fair point. How about I pick up soup and sandwiches and bring it to you? I hear lunch is one of the three meals in the day you're supposed to be consuming."

"Where'd you hear that?"

"The town cryer. It's all he talks about at top volume."

I chuckle. "Speaking of top volume, I met Dwight's dad. He's quite the talker. And did you know that Dwight has a girlfriend?"

Logan's voice is soothing, especially when he allows a two-way conversation, unlike the gentlemen I just left. "You played along, right? You didn't tell his dad Dwight made her up, did you?"

I gape at my phone, hoping I heard him wrong. "What are you talking about? Dwight made up a girlfriend?"

"Ariana. She's got blonde hair and chickens in her backyard. She makes a living as an online teacher, and I think her favorite dessert is... I want to say chocolate caramel candy bars?"

I let out a full-bellied laugh at the wealth of details put into this lie. "And she doesn't exist?"

"Never existed. I think she's out of town at a conference this week, coincidentally the same week Dwight's father came into town."

"That is quite the coincidence. My gosh, I had no idea. Their love sounds like a match made in heaven."

"Or Dwight's imagination."

"One and the same."

Logan laughs airily as I pull onto the main road. "How is Kurt?"

"Loud. Loud and proud of his boy. It would be sweet if he didn't talk nonstop. I learned about Dwight's first day of kindergarten, every great thing his son's ever done, and that the apple doesn't fall far from the tree."

Logan is happy to commiserate. "Oh, I caught the tail end of it yesterday when Kurt came to sit with Dwight at the station. Did you know that his son prefers to read the paper rather than books? Did you know that Dwight is allergic almonds? Because all of that is going in the completely useless file of things I now know about Dwight."

I slam on my breaks as my heartrate spikes. "Dwight is allergic to almonds?"

"And pine nuts and walnuts, but not peanuts, interestingly enough. Funny how the word 'interesting' loses all meaning when people start talking at length about their adult child's allergies."

I turn the car around, speeding far over the thirty-five miles per hour I am supposed to be going down the main thoroughfare. "I gave him a cupcake! Logan, if I tell you to call an ambulance, send them to Dwight's house!"

I speed with a lead foot toward Dwight's bungalow, picking out the shrubberies that flagged the property when I first visited. "Dwight!" I shout before my foot is on the driveway. "Dwight!" I race up the porch and don't bother knocking. I throw open the door, grateful no one locks anything in this town. Kurt and Dwight make noises of surprise, but one of them is muffled by a bite of cupcake.

My heart leaps into my throat as I rush inside and knock the small pink box from Dwight's hands. "Spit it out! Dwight, it has almond extract in it! I didn't realize!"

It's then that an allergic reaction begins to sweep over the man whose day I was trying to make better, but it is about to get infinitely worse.

23

ANGRY BALLERINA

"I didn't know," I tell Logan for the dozenth time since we arrived at the emergency room.

Logan cups my shoulder, his arm affixed around me as we sit in the waiting room. "I know, Miss Charlotte. You don't have to convince me of anything. I know who you are."

I should be relieved, but I'm nowhere near ready to feel even a smidge of elation. I need to know that Dwight is okay. That I didn't ruin his life, or worse, end it prematurely.

I wring my hands, anxiety peaking until Dwight himself comes around the corner with his father by his side.

I leap up with wide eyes. "Dwight! I'm so sorry! Are you okay?"

Kurt holds his hand up. "My son is going to be just fine.

He's going to take it easy tonight, though. I'll be taking him home so he can rest. They gave him enough medicine to stop the reaction, but he really should rest."

"I'm so sorry. I had no idea you were allergic to almonds, Dwight. I should have asked! I should have put that on the website. I will! From now on, all allergens will be listed on the website."

Dwight's tongue is too big for his mouth, but he gives speaking the old college try. "Ith okay, Tharlotte. Oo didn't know."

Kurt pats my head, effectively forgiving and dismissing me so he can take his son home. "I've got it from here."

Self-loathing floods me, even as I watch the two walk out of the emergency room. Logan holds me upright, bolstering me enough that I don't collapse on the spot under the weight of my regret.

Logan kisses the back of my hand. "Let's get you home. I'll package up and transport the cupcakes, and I'll make sure there's a sign for the almond extract on the dessert table."

I shake my head, though I'm grateful for the help. "No. I need to get my hands on a broom. I don't want to sit at home. I'll drive myself crazy. Too much going on in my head. I want to be helpful, especially after I just hurt someone. Cleaning up Jeanette's business seems the way to do that."

Logan purses his lips. I can tell he doesn't like this idea, but he goes along with what I want because we both know it is my decision to make.

He follows me to the Bravery Bakery, where none other than Madame Bartholomew is waiting for me outside my shop.

"Good afternoon, Madame Bartholomew. Anything I can help you with?" Logan offers, taking the spotlight off me, since I am the person at whom she is glaring.

She doesn't address Logan; only me. "What do you have against Dwight? Sure, he's a little different, but to poison him? You should be ashamed of yourself! You should be locked up!"

I don't speak in my defense. I don't even marvel at how quick word travels in this town. My mouth hangs open like a hapless guppy as I try to find the right words to say.

Logan jumps in, not nearly as tongue-tied as I am. "Charlotte did no such thing. She didn't know Dwight has a nut allergy. And what possible benefit could there be in her poisoning him?"

Madame Bartholomew draws herself up sanctimoniously. "All I know is that Dwight was brought in because she accused him of trashing her business, which he would never do. Then when you didn't arrest him, Logan, because it clearly wasn't Dwight, she took him down a different way. Permanently!"

I cup my hand over my mouth, shocked and horrified that my character hasn't afforded me the benefit of the doubt to grant me at least a conversation to defend myself.

Though, if I was in Madame Bartholomew's shoes, I might be drawn to the same conclusion.

"I'm the one who called the ambulance," I tell the woman who couldn't hate me more. "The second I realized what happened, I made sure to get him medical attention. If I was trying to kill him, I would have sat back and done nothing."

"All part of your act of innocence. Don't think I didn't catch that Jeanette's business was ransacked again. Interesting that you've been poking around in there. Mighty fine way to discover any valuables you missed the first time. It wasn't enough to put Jeanette in a coma. You had to steal every last bit of her precious gems, too?"

Logan tilts his head to the side, his body stiffening. "How did you hear that the precious gems went missing?"

Madame Bartholomew glares at Logan. "I happen to know that Jeanette has been threatened over that fountain before. Recently, in fact. She told me about it the evening before her body was found."

"The evening before?" Logan inquires. "When did you speak with her last?"

Madame Bartholomew harrumphs and pulls out her phone. "Around seven o'clock. A person wanted to buy the fountain earlier that day, but started haggling on the price, saying she wanted it, but it wasn't worth that much. Jeanette told her the gems were real, and that's why it was priced higher than the other fountains in the store. She yelled at Jeanette and then left. I'm guessing whoever it is that did this marched right back in and attacked her right after we hung up." Madame Bartholomew snarls at me.

I gape at her, wondering how this day could get any worse. "So, a woman yelled at Jeanette, and you assume I'm that woman? Why me?"

Madame Bartholomew's voice reaches a shriek. "Because you want Jeanette's storefront!"

"No, I don't! Even if she offered it to me at no cost, I don't know the first thing about running a storefront. I've got my hands full with the clients I have now. I'm not looking to expand. That's all way far down the road, if it ever happens."

Madame Bartholomew looks like she could spit nails, especially now that the reason for her hating me has been diffused by a simple explanation for which she never thought to ask.

I will not cry in front of this woman.

I raise my chin, gathering myself as much as I am able. "If you'll excuse me, I'm going to start cleaning Jeanette's store all over again. She matters to you, yes. But she also matters to me. Instead of accusing people, I'm going to put my energy into helping my friend."

Madame Bartholomew keeps her sanctimoniously stiff stature as I pass, leaving Logan behind so he can ask her for more details about the argument she overheard with said woman who was more interested in getting a deal than in playing fair with the store owner.

I take my time walking through my bakery to Jeanette's

storefront. The broom is exactly where I left it, as is the mess from the second burglary.

I hate that I hurt Dwight. I also hate that so much circumstantial evidence points directly at me, and my character isn't enough to give some people the benefit of the doubt when presented with fragments of the whole story.

Logan is silent when he comes into Sweetwater Fountains through the back entrance. He drags the garbage over and starts throwing concrete chunks into the bin, saving any bits with gems that might be valuable or reusable.

We don't talk; we don't need to. He knows my heart is heavy. Dissecting the reasons why won't lighten the load even an ounce. So, he sticks close with his calming presence, letting me deal with my sadness in silence because he knows I am capable of giving myself my own pep talk when I am ready to receive it.

It's nice to have someone in my life who knows how to be good to me.

Ten minutes later, my spine stiffens when Madame Bartholomew enters in through the same way. She also doesn't speak, but starts righting felled displays, and hanging necklaces back on the rack in a pleasing order. There is decidedly less hostility radiating off her. She doesn't speak, but every now and then, she catches my eye and gives me a silent nod.

I guess Logan must have said something to convince her that I had nothing to do with any of this.

I don't need an apology. I need to not be hated and accused when I'm already down for the count.

And I also need help cleaning up Jeanette's store. When she gets back on her feet, she deserves a grand reopening that she doesn't have to break her back to pull off.

Madame Bartholomew, Logan, and I work in silence for the next hour, making far more progress than I could have alone. When Logan speaks, it's to tell me that the surprise party will be starting soon, so he needs to transport the cupcakes.

I gnaw on my lower lip as Madame Bartholomew comes toward me, even after Logan has invited her to leave with him, so as not to put the two of us alone in a room together without a referee.

Madame Bartholomew holds my gaze, and for a second, I can't tell if she's going to say something nice, hurtful, or if she's going to slap me across the face. She strikes me as an angry ballerina.

She surprises me with an apology. "I didn't realize that you and Marianne were together at the time of the break-in. I trust Marianne, so I know she wouldn't lie to cover for you. I..." She takes a long breath, gathering her gumption for what I can tell is a difficult conversation for her. "I love Jeanette very much, and I love very few people. She is like a daughter to me. I lined up the dominoes in the wrong order and pushed them toward you, because I need for someone to pay for what they did to my sweet Jeanette. But I was wrong, and I'm sorry."

Maybe I should hold a grudge after all Madame Bartholomew has put me through. Maybe I should be angry and tell her off. But I am too tired for any of that.

I drop the broom and throw my arms around her thin frame, letting out a tearless sob on her dainty shoulder. "I'm scared for her, too. I'm doing all I can to make sure that whoever did this to Jeanette is put behind bars. I'm so angry that they broke in a second time; I can barely see straight!"

The hug I didn't know I needed finally finds me, releasing my frustration into the universe so I can breathe once more. The two of us hold each other until the tears run dry, all is forgotten, and I have renewed purpose in my mind.

I am determined to track down the burglar, so this never happens again.

I need to shower and change before the party, but my feet stop on their way to Jeanette's office after Madame Bartholomew leaves. Now that I know the date that Jeanette's problem customer was there (the day before I found her body) and the last time she spoke with anyone (around seven o'clock in the evening), I decide to poke my head in where it certainly doesn't belong.

Should Jeanette have a password on her computer?

Yes.

Does she?

No.

It doesn't take me long to pull up the software she uses to keep track of her receipts. The police confiscated her register, but not her laptop, which was in a drawer in her office. I flip through the files until I have the sheet of sales from that day.

I really need to take a shower and change. I don't want to cut it too close, being that I'm the one taking Marianne out, so she gets to the surprise party at the right time.

My eyes flick through the receipts until three bracelet purchases come up with different SKU numbers. I jot them down hurriedly and jog back to the storefront, matching the first one to a bracelet meant for love, and the second to a bracelet meant to bring serenity, like the one I am currently wearing. But the third is the one that raises the hair on the nape of my neck. "Gotcha."

I circle the SKU and head back to the computer so I can match the purchase with an identity.

My mouth falls open when I see the name I did not expect would be at the top of the suspect list.

Now I know who did it, and I know why. What I don't know is how I didn't see it all coming.

24

MATCHING BRACELETS

I am the worst company possible on the afternoon of my best friend's birthday. Marianne carries the entirety of the conversation because my mind keeps jumping back to the person who lied right to my face about the whole thing.

I need one piece of information confirmed, and I am certain I'll have the suspect unearthed and brought to justice before Jeanette returns to her store.

"I love having a best friend. It means I always have the option of having plans on my birthday. This is great!"

Marianne is so sweet, unaware of the shadow over my mood that keeps my smile hollow.

"One year older. Got any plans for this next year, Marianne the Wild?"

Marianne bops in the passenger's seat. "I really want to read more books than I did last year. And I want to try carnitas. I was watching a cooking show about them, and everyone looked so happy eating them."

I love her sweet little list. "Tell me more. We can make both of those things happen."

"I want to go on a roller coaster." She holds up her hands. "I know, I know. I'm too old for amusement parks. But I've never been, and I think I'm ready."

I gape at her admission. "You've never been to an amusement park?"

She shakes her head. "I wasn't a fan of screaming or crowds when I was a kid."

"I can see that. Well, we can make that happen, too."

She claps her hands together excitedly. "Maybe they'll have carnitas at the restaurant we're going to."

"Maybe. That would be fortunate, for sure." The plan is for me to drive by the library, where there is a big sign out front stretched across the grass reading "Happy Birthday, Marianne!"

I'm glad I don't have to orchestrate more than that. My mind is going a mile a minute, flicking from my best friend to the person whom I am certain is guilty of hurting Jeanette.

When I drive slowly by the library, Marianne's jaw drops. "What on earth? Is that..."

Surprise: delivered.

My best friend's hands fly over her mouth as her brows hit her hairline. "Oh my goodness! Charlotte, did you know about this? Is this for me?"

I grin, mustering a smile only for her. "The whole town is in on it. We all wanted a chance to celebrate our favorite girl."

Marianne doesn't cry demurely but instead bursts into squeals and tears, fanning her face. The moment I park, she explodes out of the car, hugging every person who greets her along the way.

Do I have a favorite literary character? I'm not sure. But I like the *Wizard of Oz*, which is also a book, so my blue and white gingham apron works just fine as I pull it from my purse and twist it around my waist, paired with red sneakers.

Dorothy. Blammo. I participated.

Once Marianne is sufficiently swept up in the hullabaloo of hugs and birthday wishes, I beeline for the one person I have been needing to see, moving past the table filled with cupcakes and the grand birthday cake that normally would give me a lift at seeing the hard work all lain out.

I don't even acknowledge the dunk tank, or the fact that Karen is in her bikini on the tiny platform, ready to be plunged into the depths whenever the next child hits their mark.

I don't remark on Carlos' perfect Darcy costume from one of Marianne's favorite novels.

Right now, I don't care about anything but getting to the bottom of this mess.

"Fisher!" I call through the crowd in the parking lot of the library. "Fisher, I have to talk to you."

The people do not part for me, so I have to worm my way through the smiles, forgetting to don my own.

When I reach my friend, I hold onto his wrist. "Fisher, what time was your date with Lydia?"

Fisher blinks at me. "I'm taking her out tomorrow. I think we said five o'clock after our shifts end. Why?"

I shake my head. "Not tomorrow's date. The first one. Was it in the evening?"

Fisher's brows pinch. "What's this about? You look ready to come out of your skin; you're so intense."

I close my eyes, hoping the right words come to me. I'm so near to putting a pin in this burglary. I need to know how this final piece fits before I can be certain. "What time were you two together on your first date, Fisher?"

My friend purses his lips before replying. "I took her out to lunch, but it was a two-hour drive. We had a great time. It would have gone longer, but she said she needed to take care of something, so I took her back. I thought she was blowing me off, but she said yes to a second date, so she probably had an errand to run that evening or something."

I squeeze his hand. "Think real hard back to your date. Was Lydia wearing a bracelet? Orange and green gemstones?" I hold up my wrist. "Like this one, but with orange in there, too?"

Fisher's mouth screws to the side. "I'm not sure about

the color, but yeah, I think she was wearing a bracelet. When I held her hand, I saw it. She was wearing a necklace, too. I don't remember what it looked like, though."

I am winded, but I can't afford to lose focus so near the finish line. "Thanks, Fisher. That's exactly what I needed to hear."

I'd written Lydia off my list of suspects because I'd assumed her date with Fisher had taken place in the evening. But if she was with him in the middle of the day, then that left her open to have been at Sweetwater Fountains in the morning to buy the bracelet to bring good luck. Then Lydia could have come back in the evening, when her date wasn't the movie star of her dreams. That's when she unleashed her frustrations with the universe on poor Jeanette.

But just when I am sure I have all the evidence I need to turn into Logan, Lydia herself comes up beside Fisher, fixing me with a critical eye. "You interested in my jewelry, Charlotte? Why is that?"

I debate between outright accusing her in the middle of the birthday party or letting the police handle it.

Marianne's party is not the setting for a citizen's arrest, so I hold up my hands. "You're very stylish, Lydia. Any chance you have a bracelet with green and orange gemstones? I thought I saw you wearing one, but I can't remember. I was thinking of getting something similar, but I don't want to be too matchy-matchy."

Lydia doesn't fall for my dodge for a second. "Is that

so?" She flips her black hair over her shoulder, handing Fisher a drink. "No, I don't have anything like that."

I tilt my head to the side, realizing that she knows I'm onto her. "You didn't buy a bracelet from Sweetwater Fountains that brings good luck?"

Lydia scoffs. "As if anything in that store is real. A bunch of nonsense. Luck is what you make of it. Jeanette sells wishes, not realities. That store should come with a warning label."

I hold myself back from outright accusing her, even though we both know she is the one who purchased said bracelet at a time when she was not with Fisher, and then denied the whole thing.

Lydia wanted the bracelet to bring her good luck. When it didn't, she came back after her date and yelled at Jeanette, attacking and robbing her. Lydia needs more capital if she's going to open her restaurant drive-thru branch in Sweetwater Falls, so she came back to the store for a second robbery to take the gems that might be of any value to resell.

I know she stole from Sweetwater Fountains.

Lydia knows I know she stole from Sweetwater Fountains.

We are locked in a stalemate, a silent game of chicken where she knows I won't ruin Marianne's party with a scandal, and also that I won't let her leave my sight, unless it is in handcuffs.

I release my friend and step back, letting the crowd put

distance between us so I can gather my bearings enough to handle what needs to happen next. "I'm going to see to the birthday girl. Later, guys."

I feel Lydia's eyes on me as I make my way not to Marianne, but to Logan, who has the authority to bring Lydia to justice.

But before I make it to my boyfriend's side, I am pushed from the crowd, in through the front doors of the library, where the party is most certainly not taking place.

I barely get out an "Oof!" of surprise before a woman's fist clocks me across the face.

If I wasn't sure Lydia was the culprit before, I certainly am now.

I had nothing against Lydia until it became apparent to me that she was at fault for putting Jeanette in the hospital and stealing from Sweetwater Fountains. But now that the receptionist for The Snuggle Inn has punched me across the face, I have a little more than just suspicion that she is not the best of people to have roaming the streets of Sweetwater Falls.

"Whatever you think you know, you'll keep your mouth shut about!" Lydia shouts at me, and then grabs the front of my shirt so she can snarl in my throbbing face. "You don't know anything, so you'll not go running off to your little boyfriend!"

Maybe a smarter person would play along, shrinking under her rage, but I have never been accused of superior self-preservation. "You bought a bracelet from

Jeanette, and when it didn't bring you luck, you chewed her out for it. Then you attacked her and stole from the register!" My face is throbbing, but I don't hold back. "You came back with tools to dig out those precious gems, too!"

Lydia's hands curl around my throat, squeezing as if that will make it all not true. "You have no idea how hard I've worked, how diligently I've scrimped and saved to get enough money to open the business of my dreams! If I'd had just a little luck, I would have been able to afford the buy-in fee for the franchise! I could be a manager right now!" She squeezes harder, making my eyes bug. "Do you have any idea how beneath me it is to answer a phone all the livelong day? I could be running that place! Any place! Give me a business, and I can run it!"

I can't pry her fingers from my throat, so I reach out for anything that might prove useful. When Lydia slams my back to the circulation desk in the empty library, my arms flail until my hand lands on a stack of books.

I grab one up with clumsy fingers, smacking it to the side of Lydia's forehead.

The impact is just enough to loosen her grip, giving me the chance to duck away and run for the exit.

Thank goodness for hardcover books.

I don't make it two steps before Lydia tackles me to the ground, shrieking her rage into the echoey library. "Jeanette practically gave you that kitchen. Gave it to you! She knew I wanted it! I deserve it! That bracelet was supposed to give me luck, but when I showed up to the date to meet the mystery man, it was Fisher!"

I kick at her, elbowing and contorting to try to get her off me. "Do you hear yourself? Fisher is a catch! That is good luck, to have caught the eye of someone as wonderful as him!"

She scoffs, as if Fisher is beneath her.

White-hot anger curdles my blood as I fight to get Lydia off me. I know I can't make it to the door to flag for help. She's determined, and far stronger than I was anticipating.

I reach up, my arm fishing around for anything on the reception desk that might prove useful.

When my fingers close on the desktop amethyst fountain I bought from Jeanette months ago to give to Marianne for Christmas, I realize that justice is about to be served.

The fountain dumps water down my arm as I bring it over the edge, cracking Lydia over the head with it.

Finally, Jeanette's attacker and mine slumps to the floor. All the fight drains out of her in a breath.

I scramble to my feet, terrified and motivated to get out of there as fast as my feet will carry me. No longer do I care about bringing drama into the thick of Marianne's birthday. I only care that I live to see her next birthday, so I can make this up to her.

I burst out of the library, shouting at the top of my lungs, "I found the person who attacked Jeanette!"

The party guests turn to me as one, freezing until Logan breaks them out of their shock. He runs through the crowd to my side, curling one arm around my waist as he pokes his head into the library. "Lydia?" He angles his chin over his shoulder to call for backup. "Dad! Wayne! Get in here!"

The residents of Sweetwater Falls close in, each of them wanting a peek into the library so they can see just who is at fault for attacking one of their beloved.

Luckily, the sheriff shuts them out, leaving the five of us in the building without an audience.

I grip Logan's arm. "It's Lydia. She confessed the whole thing to me. Tried to choke me out." My chest heaves as blessed oxygen floods my system. "I got away. I got away."

The sheriff fixes me with a serious look. "What did she confess, exactly?"

"I have the receipt!" I say, getting the evidence out of order. "Lydia wants to open a drive-thru in Sweetwater Falls. A chain store burger joint. She asked Jeanette for the space I rent, but Jeanette said no. Lydia bought a lucky bracelet from Sweetwater Fountains, but when her date was Fisher instead of some mystery hunk, she came back after her date and yelled at Jeanette. She's the one who attacked Jeanette! Then she stole from the register because she needed more money to open her branch."

Logan pulls me to his side, steadying me as the rest comes out in a gust.

"That's why she returned to the scene of the crime!

That's how the precious gems went missing! Lydia wanted more valuables to bolster her business plan."

The sheriff most likely has a million more questions, but that's all the information I have, or can gather at the moment, until another burst comes out of me. "I found the receipt on Jeanette's computer! It places Lydia at Sweetwater Fountains on the day of the first break-in!"

The sheriff cups my shoulder, fixing his steady gaze on my sweaty features. "All you had to tell me was she attacked you, and I would have slapped on the cuffs. The fact that she might have hurt Jeanette, too?" He motions to Wayne to do the job of arresting Lydia once she comes to. "You won't have to worry about this one ever again, Charlotte."

Logan doesn't let go of me, even after Lydia wakes up to find herself being arrested for her crimes. His arms stay around me as Lydia is marched out past the whole of Sweetwater Falls, so that everyone can see that I harbor nothing but gratitude for Jeanette and all she's done for me.

My hand bunches in the front of Logan's green polo shirt. "Tell me it's over," I whisper as the doors close, leaving us in the quiet of the empty library.

Logan brings my fingers to his lips so he can kiss the backs of my knuckles. "Actually, I think now Marianne's party can finally begin."

25

GRAND REOPENING

The moment Jeanette woke from her coma and was cleared to go back home, it's as if a curse was lifted from the whole of Sweetwater Falls. The birds began singing their late-spring song. The squirrels chased each other for the best nut on the block. The people started walking down the streets with an extra pep in their step.

Because if Jeanette is back, that means it's time for the town's second party inside a month.

The Grand Reopening of Sweetwater Fountains isn't something any of us can talk Jeanette into postponing. I even sat her down and told her to go slower. Coming back full throttle certainly cannot be the doctor's orders.

"Are you sure you're ready for this?" I ask Jeanette the morning of her big day.

Her red waist-length flowing hair has been braided by

Aunt Winnie. Her nails have been painted by Marianne. Her seventies-style dress is new—a gift from Betty.

But most radiant of all is Jeanette herself, clad in a pretty apron that Madame Bartholomew embroidered herself.

We caution Jeanette to go slow before she opens the doors, but she has been a tornado of constant motion for weeks now. She was able to replenish her store from the stock she had in storage lined on shelves in the back, but ever since she's been on her feet, her hands have been crafting and molding new creations, giving the entire storefront a vibrancy that draws my eye every time I enter, which is often.

Aunt Winnie stands at the front door, getting the small table of drinks set up. A glass of sparkling water will be gifted to every customer when they come to the grand reopening of Sweetwater Fountains.

Marianne sets her new purse behind the register, tucking the rare edition copy of Jane Austen's *Emma* into the special fold designed to hold a book.

Did I know they sold purses with a compartment meant to carry a book inside? No, I did not. But after Lydia was taken away, Carlos and I were able to give Marianne her birthday gifts—a new purse that will keep her books' pages from crinkling while she goes about her day from me, with a rare edition copy of *Emma* tucked inside from Carlos.

I'm really glad we teamed up on that.

Marianne hasn't been resentful in the least that her birthday had a little too much surprise to it. No one scheduled an arrest, but that's exactly what happened, and we're all grateful the worst is behind us.

Lydia wasted no time confessing to the crime once she was brought in after attacking me. That, coupled with the evidence found in her home, is going to put her behind bars for quite some time.

The stolen jewels and cash were returned to Jeanette, but Fisher's heart is still tucked in Lydia's pocket.

I stopped by to see Fisher last night, checking on the man who harbored a crush on a woman that turned out to be a felon behind the scenes. I brought him a cupcake, which broke the ice and opened the door for him to unload the feelings that come to a crash when something like this occurs.

I stayed for three hours, letting him vent about his dashed hopes that he and Lydia might become something real and worth holding onto.

Betty bumps her elbow to mine, bringing me back to the present. "Charlotte, I'm not sure this is enough." She motions to the table on the opposite side of the entrance from Aunt Winnie's sparkling water table, which is laden with our offering to help the grand reopening be a big success.

"I brought out a hundred. That should be enough for a few hours, don't you think?"

Betty shakes her head, motioning to the store's picture window. "Take a look at the line."

The shades are drawn while we finish prepping for the big reveal, so I come forward, peeking my nose around the edge of the shade.

My eyes widen as I step back. "Are you kidding me? Jeanette, the entire town has shown up for this! I need to bring out more mini cupcakes, Betty. Hold on." I tap on the glass, garnering the attention of the man in a mascot costume, dressed as a treasure chest. I give him a thumb's up to let him know it's nearly showtime.

I'm not sure how a giant treasure chest ties into the fountain store's aesthetic, but I'm grateful Dwight agreed to dress up for the occasion to entertain the people in line.

Beside the dancing treasure chest is a man dressed as a giant book, shaking hands with children in the sunshine.

I still can't believe that Kurt agreed to move back to Sweetwater Falls to be closer to his son. I love that they have each other.

Betty frets from my left. "Charlotte, we need more cupcakes!"

"On it!" I jerk back from the window.

I've never sold mini cupcakes before, but it seemed the perfect thing to offer in show of support to the woman who took a chance on me.

Madame Bartholomew shoos me to the back. "Hurry! I'm opening the doors at nine o'clock exactly. That's fifteen seconds from now!"

I hop with a squeak and race to the Bravery Bakery through the back door behind the register. My red sneakers carry me to the counter, where just this morning, I chastised myself for making far too many mini cupcakes, misjudging the amount of batter needed to make them.

I load up several dozen in a box to take out and put under the table for Betty to pass out, knowing I've well surpassed the fifteen-second deadline.

I can hear the crowd filtering in, ready to marvel at the new pieces Jeanette has made since getting back on her feet.

While the bracelet may not have brought Lydia good luck, it seems the only good fortune needed is the love and support of the wonderful people in Sweetwater Falls.

And perhaps, a cupcake or two.

The End.

Love the book?

Leave a review!

26

KEY LIME KILLER PREVIEW

Enjoy a Free Preview of *Key Lime Killer*—Book Ten in the Cupcake Crimes Series.

harity Drive Mess

Marianne's eyes are wide, yet I know she hasn't had a lick of caffeine this morning. "I thought the signs went up yesterday. How..."

I could finish her thought aloud, but I don't need to. How, indeed. How had a cozy small town come up with so many items to be donated in such a short time? How many items are there? My mind cannot quantify the mess, but that is exactly what we signed on to do. With Marianne's keen organizational mind and my work ethic, I didn't think we would have any problem helping to sort out the donations for the charity drive.

I clearly underestimated how much stuff the people of Sweetwater Falls want to get rid of.

There are a few enormous piles that stretch taller than my five-foot-eleven inches, and many that are wide enough to need navigational assistance to maneuver. There are things in black garbage bags, things in small white grocery bags, and things in overflowing boxes, each stacked and toppling because more is coming in than can be organized into categories. The few volunteers that mill about seem aimless, which I completely understand. My mind is on the verge of shorting out, due to the flood of stuff.

I have no idea where to begin when I walk further into the high school gymnasium. Being that the school is closed for the summer, we have the whole space to set up some sort of organizational system for optimum shopping.

And we have less than two weeks to do it.

When the door swings open behind us, Frank shuffles inside with a large box in his arms. "Don't mind me. Just dropping off a few things for the drive."

I want to tell my friend, who is the owner and operator of the Nosy Newsy, to turn right back around. There is no way the literal mountain of clothes to my left and mishmash of home furnishings to my right need to grow even the slightest bit taller.

Instead of bolting for the parking lot so I don't have to deal with this chaos, I wave to my great-aunt Winifred, who is busying herself sorting clothes. She looks up at me, her sea-green eyes coming into focus at my presence. "Oh, Charlotte! Just in time. I was thinking... I can't remember now. I'm in the haze." She holds her arms out as if she is a mindless mummy. Her shoulder-length silver curly hair swishes from side to side while she teeters to add to the theatrics.

My eyes are wide as I walk toward my great-aunt in all of her five-feet-tall cuteness. "This is a far larger project than I realized. Is it like this every year?"

Aunt Winifred shakes her head. "We didn't have a charity drive last year, so I think this is two years' worth of accumulated stuff. The charity drive is everyone's reminder to go through their things and get rid of what they're not using. But we didn't get that reminder last year, so it appears the drive is bursting at the seams."

Marianne balks at the madness, only she doesn't have the glazed-over look most of the volunteers wear. On the contrary, she appears enthralled, ready to tackle the challenge of a lifetime.

Thank goodness for people like Marianne.

And apparently, Rip, the Town Selectman, who loves a

good event and the elbow grease that goes into it. He trots in from the hallway, blowing a whistle he's got hanging around his neck. The sound echoes through the cavernous gymnasium. "Three cheers for the new volunteers! Hip-hip!"

The lackluster "Hooray" coming from the handful of volunteers around us does not offer the intended cheer, but it's the thought that counts, I suppose.

Rip shakes his head with a goofy grin curving the corners of his mouth. He tucks his red polo shirt into his slightly pooched waistline as he jogs over to us. His salt-and-pepper hair is firmly fixed in place with a hard shellac of hairspray. The smile on his rounded face makes him look like Santa Claus' dapper cousin, if his jolliness is any indication. "Good morning, ladies. How long do I have you for?"

Marianne had made it clear on the phone with me that she needed to sort books at noon today, so she doesn't fall behind, but after seeing the project lain out before her, she answers with a hearty, "You've got me all day, Rip. I am here for this." Her eyes are still wide, her chocolate-colored pixie-short hair swishing around her cheekbones as her head turns this way and that. She is a slight little thing, but she looks like a sturdy pioneer at the beginning of a trail she cannot wait to blaze.

My neck shrinks when I reply, "You've got me for two hours. After that, I need to get to the bakery."

Or, get *back* to the bakery, as it were. I started out my day at six this morning, baking cupcakes at the Bravery Bakery—specializing in the world's best honey cakes. It's my dream job, and being that the bakery is all mine, I can't leave my dream unattended on a whim.

Though, seeing this mammoth mess, the urge is strong to do exactly that. I don't like to leave projects unfinished, and there doesn't seem to be an end in sight for this one.

Marianne is usually my meek friend who doesn't take charge willy-nilly. But today, she looks taller, unwilling to quiet her voice when she knows it is useful. "I'm thinking you need someone in charge of sorting the household items." She motions to the far-left wall. "We need tables up first, so we can set the things where they'll need to go instead of shuffling them around in piles. Also, we'll need more real estate. What do you think about collapsing the bleachers to make more room for tables?"

Rip scratches his head, turning to survey the bleachers. "Where would people sit while they eat their hot dogs?"

Of course this isn't just a simple charity drive. There will be a picnic lunch and live music. Rip doesn't do things halfway.

Marianne jerks her thumb to the exit. "Can we move the food outside and set up picnic blankets instead of using the bleachers?"

He clasps his hands together, impossibly more cheerful at her suggestion. "A citywide picnic? That sounds like the best idea I've ever heard! And picnic blankets instead of tables and chairs will be far easier to set up and tear down. I love it!"

Marianne nods once. "Sounds good. Where are the long tables, Rip?"

Rip laughs like a man who appreciates the simple joys in life as he throws his arms around Marianne. "I'm so glad you're here. Yes, that's fantastic. If you like, you can help me bring out the long tables and get them set up. Then I'm turning you loose on household items. No one seems to want to tackle that this morning."

Marianne cracks her knuckles like a boxer gearing up for the match of a lifetime. "I've got this, Rip. But I'm keeping Charlotte with me. I'll need a helper."

Rip salutes Marianne, and I love everything about the exchange—especially that I don't have to make decisions about what needs to happen first. It's all a jumbled mess to me.

Marianne points in Aunt Winnie's direction. "The clothing sorters need to each take a bag and sort the contents into the various piles. I see they're just searching for one category of clothing and leaving the rest. That means each bag will be gone through four times (men's, women's, children's, and bedding). Unnecessary."

Rip holds up his finger enthusiastically. "On it! I'll redirect the clothing volunteers. Charlotte, can you help Marianne with the tables?"

I nod, and Rip trots off to the clothing area. "You know, Rip is one of a kind. He's happy to take charge and happy to let others call the shots if they can do it better."

"Oh, he's fantastic." Marianne motions to the hallway. "Let's get cracking. If I've got you for two hours, I want every bit of work you've got until you walk out that door."

I salute her because I love the idea of not being in charge for two whole hours. I'm not naturally an assertive person, so being the decisionmaker for my business stretches a muscle I didn't realize I had at the ready. When I can give that muscle a rest and just be the employee, it is a relief I will not push aside.

Marianne and I make quick work of setting up a row of long rectangular tables that stretch from the front of the gymnasium to the back. It's probably not a good sign that I am already sweating, but I keep my grunts and groans silent, so as not to dampen Marianne's forward motion. She grabs up Rip's abandoned clipboard and tears a few sheets from his notepad, scribbling on them before she makes her way to the row of tables. "Here," she says, taping a paper to one table, then moving to the next. "These are the categories, labeled so we don't get confused. Start with one box and don't put it down until it's been emptied. If you're not sure where it should go, set it on the Miscellaneous table, but let's not get precious about the piles. Guessing wrong is fine. We don't want the Miscellaneous table overflowing by the end." When she catches me eyeing the avalanche of items to sort, she puts herself in my eyeline. "Focus on one box at a time, otherwise we'll get overwhelmed."

Marianne is usually my sweet, softspoken bestie, but today she is large and in charge. I love it, so I don't waste a second before I comply with her orders.

"On it!" I sing, pretending I am not daunted by this task in the least. I pick up the nearest box, uncertain what a few of the items that greet me actually are. But Marianne's words ring in my head that it's better to guess wrong than to dawdle over getting everything perfect.

Tin kettle.

Cast-iron skillet half-covered in rust.

Salt and pepper shakers.

Plastic planters.

I sort everything as quick as I can onto the tables that Marianne was smart enough to label. She used vague enough specifications that I don't hem and haw over finding an overly specific category.

Man, she's good.

Marianne ignores her phone when it rings, keeping her eyes on her task as though it is the only thing in her mind. She is a tiny machine, but powerful and unstoppable. Her work ethic puts a fire under me, and in turn, the rest of the volunteers pick up their pace, as well.

Three boxes are broken down and thrown into the garbage bin. Four. When I hit my fifth, I feel as though I have found my rhythm as I unpack the items and set them on their respective tables.

Dull kitchen knives.

Black kitchen towels.

Baseball.

Wire cutters.

Cookie jar.

The kitchen hardware items should go to my right, so I sort the other items first, and then head to the end of the row with the dull knives and the cookie jar.

I don't expect the mountain of clothing to tumble in my direction, nor do I anticipate how cumbersome the avalanche might be when it doesn't stop and refuses to make room for my steps. A volunteer shrieks an apology to the rest of us as the mountain topples, but I can't get out of the way fast enough.

The kitchen knives and the cookie jar fly from my hands when I am pushed sideways by a snowman-sized bundle of clothing. I cringe and shout a quick, "Heads up!" scrambling to get out of the way as the knives and jar fling upward and then come crashing to the ground.

"Ah!" I grimace, shocked that I couldn't get out of there fast enough to avoid one of the knives nicking my forearm. The cookie jar crashes to the ground, shattering into pieces, and the rest of the knives stake themselves into various garments that are puddled at my feet.

Marianne gasps and runs to me, tugging me toward the

tables and away from the mess that I partially created. "Oh, Charlotte! You're bleeding!"

"It's fine," I tell her, inspecting the outside of my arm. In truth, the cut doesn't seem particularly deep, but the shock of it is still ringing through me. "The knives are scattered on the ground, though. I need to clean that up, so no one gets hurt."

Marianne types out a text on her phone. "Logan is going to take you to Urgent Care."

"I'm really okay."

My best friend isn't one to take chances with my health. "One of those knives cut you? That wound needs to be cleaned out by a professional. No arguments."

"But I only sorted a few boxes! I can do more."

Marianne eyes me, her hand on her hip while she waits for a reply text from my boyfriend. "I'm sure you can, after you go to Urgent Care, and they make sure you're not going to get an infection from the knife that cut you."

I roll my eyes like a child being told to take their medicine. "Oh, fine. At least let me clean up the mess so no one else gets hurt."

Marianne takes a handful of tissues from the package in her purse and presses them to my arm. "Okay, but that's the last thing you're doing. Then you're sitting way over there and waiting for Logan."

"I can drive myself."

Her phone chirps with a text. She straightens her posture as she exercises her authority. "You can prove that after your arm has been looked at by a medical professional."

I grumble just loud enough for her to hear that I am unhappy at leaving her to deal with the project as I make my way to the dropped knives and smashed cookie jar. I pick up the knives, though I am uncertain how many there were, so I do a thorough job of searching the pile to make sure no one has the misfortune of stepping on one if they pass by this area. My fingers are slippery as blood dribbles down my forearm and tickles my hand.

Perhaps the cut is deeper than I realized.

It's when I lift an orange dress to search it for the strewn cutlery that my movements still. I blink twice, unable to make sense of what my mind is telling me I am seeing.

"That's got to be a Halloween prop," I murmur to myself as I reach down and pick up the severed hand that looks like it belonged to a woman. It has to be the best faked appendage I've ever seen in my life, wrapped in plastic. But the second my fingers uncurl the digits of the strange item, my spine stiffens. I know what rubber props feel like, and this is not that. The skin gives, and there is bruising around the wrist where tendons and sinew stretch out like spaghetti inside the plastic.

My intake of breath is enough for Marianne to rush to my side. "You shouldn't be bothering with this, Charlotte. I'll clean up the..." But when she sees the same thing that's sent my heart rate into overdrive, I know that Marianne is rethinking her choice to volunteer at the charity drive this morning.

I turn to my best friend, eyes wide and spine tingling with the unknown. "Marianne, you need to call the police. I think there's been a murder."

Read *Key Lime Killer* by Molly Maple today!

FUNFETTI CUPCAKE RECIPE

Yield: 12 Cupcakes

"Marianne had funfetti every year growing up, packed with so many colorful sprinkles, it had more sprinkles than frosting."

-Funfetti Feud, by Molly Maple

For the Cupcake:

½ cup unsalted butter at room temperature

¾ cup granulated sugar

½ cup whole milk

2 eggs at room temperature

1 tsp pure vanilla extract

½ tsp almond extract

1 ½ cups all-purpose flour

1 tsp baking powder

½ tsp salt

½ cup rainbow sprinkles

Instructions for the Cupcake:

1. Preheat the oven to 350°F.
2. Using a stand mixer, cream ½ cup unsalted butter and ¾ cup granulated sugar in a large mixing bowl.
3. Mix in ½ cup whole milk.
4. Add eggs one at a time and beat until fluffy and light in color.
5. Add 1 tsp pure vanilla extract and ½ tsp almond extract. Mix until well combined.
6. In a medium bowl, sift together 1 ½ cups all-purpose flour, 1 tsp baking powder, and ½ tsp salt.
7. Slowly fold rainbow sprinkles into batter until just combined. Do not overmix.
8. Divide the batter into your 12-count lined cupcake pan, filling each one 2/3 the way full.
9. Bake for 15-20 minutes at 350°F, or until a toothpick inserted in the center comes out clean.
10. Let them cool in the pan for 10 minutes, then transfer to a cooling rack. Cool to room temperature before frosting.

Ingredients for the Vanilla Buttercream Frosting:

¾ cup unsalted butter, softened

3 cups confectioner's sugar

1 tsp vanilla extract

¼ tsp almond extract

1-2 Tbsp milk, as needed

Rainbow sprinkles for topping

Instructions for the Vanilla Buttercream Frosting:

1. Beat ¾ cup unsalted butter in a stand mixer until fluffy and light in color (2-3 minutes on medium-high speed).
2. Add half the confectioner's sugar with 1 tsp vanilla extract. Mix until fluffy.
3. Add the other half of the confectioner's sugar with ¼ tsp almond extract. Mix until fluffy.
4. Add an additional Tablespoon or two of milk as needed. Mix until fluffy and firm enough to pipe.
5. Top with rainbow sprinkles.

ABOUT THE AUTHOR

Author Molly Maple believes in the magic of hot tea and the romance of rainy days.

She is a fan of all desserts, but cupcakes have a special place in her heart. Molly spends her days searching for fresh air, and her evenings reading in front of a fireplace.

Molly Maple is a pen name for USA Today bestselling fantasy author Mary E. Twomey, and contemporary romance author Tuesday Embers.

Visit her online at www.MollyMapleMysteries.com. Sign up for her newsletter to be alerted when her next new release is coming.